About the

Kerry Carter used to be an administrator at the University of York, England where she had worked for over thirty years. She took early retirement through ill health when she finally admitted defeat to the debilitating illness, multiple sclerosis. Diagnosed with MS in 2001, she was determined to do a few things before her health got too bad, including scuba diving and swimming with manatees in Florida. After her work life ended, Kerry decided to write a book. She couldn't type any more, so she had to use voice activated software to write what she was speaking. *Decisions* is the result.

Decisions

Kerry Carter

Decisions

Vanguard Press

VANGUARD PAPERBACK

© Copyright 2023
Kerry Carter

A CIP catalogue record for this title is
available from the British Library.

ISBN 978 1 80016 863 3

Vanguard Press is an imprint of
Pegasus Elliot Mackenzie Publishers Ltd.
www.pegasuspublishers.com

First Published in 2023

Vanguard Press
Sheraton House Castle Park
Cambridge England

Printed & Bound in Great Britain

For John and the never-ending supply of love and care.

I'd like to thank all my family, for believing in me. I knew I had a book in me somewhere, but it's only taken forty years to make an appearance!

Chapter 1

Decisions, decisions. What shall I have for lunch? I might get a sandwich from Scoffs, the deli across the road, but what filling? I should pick something really healthy like a turkey salad (boring). Or maybe I'll go for what I really want which is a double cheeseburger and large fries from McDonald's (oh gosh, yes please). That won't help the diet though. God, this is the problem with working in the city centre, just too many choices.

"Sasha, what are you having for lunch?"

"Hmmm, I'm not too sure. I think I might just get a sandwich from M&S," Sasha replied, putting on some lipstick as she spoke.

"OK, I'll come with you."

Sasha had been my best friend since my first day at primary school. At first, I never really spent any time with her, being more interested in hanging upside down on the climbing frame and playing kiss chase with the boys. When we started secondary school, we were both in the same class and we started to spend more time with each other. She lived just round the corner from me so it was easy to walk round to her house and her to mine.

We spent our time listening to music, watching TV and doing an awful lot of laughing. Many a time Sasha had lent me a shoulder to cry on when I'd been dumped by yet another boyfriend. I'd like to say that I offered the same for Sasha, but she was the dumper more often than not, not the dumpee. We grew up together, cried together, laughed together and had a great time together. She's my best friend and I don't know what I'd do without her.

Sasha often came on holiday with us, usually somewhere in the UK, but occasionally we went abroad. We went to Spain one year when we were around seventeen, when Mum and Dad would let us have the odd drink or two (or three or four was more like it). That was the first time that Sasha and me had experienced hangovers. We felt so dreadful the next day after necking a few bottles of sangria, we said we'd never touch alcohol again! Ha! Never again, my arse!

It was just a coincidence that we both started working in the same department at the university. Sasha had already worked there for about three months before I came on the scene. Being best friends at work might make people think we would spend too much time gossiping and laughing and not getting the work done. It couldn't be further from the truth. Don't get me wrong, we had our moments when we had a good laugh, but we were both hard working and committed when we needed to be. We would flog our guts out to get things done on time. As a result, we were appreciated by the rest of the university work team and we received thanks on many occasions for the hard work we'd done.

On some days it was so quiet, Val (the department manager), would let us have a day off. She wasn't officially supposed to do this, but she believed that if we didn't have anything to do at work, we could be doing something more useful at home. This was much appreciated, but I must say that every time it happened, I ended up just having a lie in and mooching about the house all day pampering myself.

Val stuck her head round the door now. "I'm expecting a delivery of books any time soon, so keep your eye out. Give me a ring when they arrive and I'll come and collect them."

Val was my boss and you couldn't wish for anyone nicer. She was down-to-earth and had the respect from all of us who worked there. Val had been trying for years to have a baby and we had seen her going through the pain of miscarriage on three separate occasions. Now she was trying IVF and was on her second round of trying. We all had our fingers tightly crossed that it would work this time.

I put my coat on. It seemed like a nice day, but lately there had been rain showers that happened so quickly you didn't even have time to put your umbrella up. That is if you even remembered to take your umbrella, which I invariably forgot.

"Are you still up for our night out next Saturday?" asked Sasha, putting on her trendy rain mac from Coach.

"You bet I am, I can't wait," I replied, putting on my (not so trendy) coat from Leeds market. Our nights out coincided with getting paid at the end of the month and usually included a meal, drinks and a club. We always managed to drink far too much and get pretty hammered by the end of the night, wobbling back from a taxi in the early hours of the morning. Last month, during our night out, I seem to have lost the heel of one of my shoes. I haven't the foggiest idea how that came about. All I remember is that we had a brilliant night, even though I had to fork out for a new pair of shoes!

We came out of the door of the main entrance to the office and it had already started raining. Sasha had one of those trendy umbrellas where you just press a button and it goes up. Mine was the less trendy version that you put up by hand and was so cheap that any slight gust of wind blew it inside out.

We made our way through the brightly coloured myriad of umbrellas to Marks and Spencer. As we entered the store, I couldn't help glancing left and right and seeing all the things that were for sale. I really wanted to spend some time looking at the goods but I couldn't as my time was limited. I wish they made a pair of glasses, like blinkers for a horse, that made looking left and right impossible, so you couldn't tease yourself with all the things you could buy. The trip to Marks and

Spencer should have been a quick job, but I was so distracted by all of the tops and T-shirts, shorts and dresses, skirts and cardigans on offer. I found it hard to tear myself away and concentrate on what I had actually come into the store for in the first place, which was to buy a sandwich for lunch. Buying clothes would be bad news from a savings point of view as I was trying to save money for our planned trip to Menorca in June.

"Oooh look, they've got the summer stock in. I really need to buy some more T-shirts to go away on holiday but I guess I should look at the weekend when I've got more time to do it justice."

Sasha was equally distracted. "Hey, look at these bags. They would be fantastic for taking to the beach. You could keep all your necessary bits inside it like a book, suncream, sunglasses and a bit of money. And they're plenty big enough to put a towel in as well."

"Look at these shorts. They would look fantastic on you with your figure, but I'd look like a beached whale in them. No, even worse, a white beached whale."

"Don't be so hard on yourself, you've got a gorgeous figure," Sasha commented while rifling through a clothes rail of teeny tiny shorts.

That's another thing about us. We're like chalk and cheese to look at. Sasha is petite, slim and has a figure to die for. Whereas I'm tall, well-built and curvaceous. I suppose my redeeming feature is that I've got much bigger boobs, which in their own right attract attention from the boys, but they do tend to get in the way sometimes.

I'm always on a diet of some kind. Weight Watchers, SlimFast, the Atkins diet, Mindful Chef, I could go on. You name it, I've tried it, sometimes with some success. With others, though, I seem to end up putting more weight on. Let's face it, I'm not cut out to be a glorious, sylph-like, sex goddess. Sasha says I should just learn to love my curves and stop beating myself up about it. Easy for her to say. She's about three stone lighter than me.

I took a quick glance at my watch. "We'd better get a sandwich quick. Lunch time is nearly over. We've got totally absorbed looking at a holiday clothes and not the thing we came to do in the first place." We hung the clothes we were holding back on to the racks. They'll have to wait until Saturday.

We made our way to the sandwich section of the store and quickly made our purchases. Sasha had chosen a chicken salad sandwich and I selected a healthy prawn salad in an effort to lose a bit more weight before the holiday. I chose to ignore the chocolate brownie I bought for my pudding.

When we got to the office, a fair pile of work had accumulated and we set about working steadily through the letters, tables and reports.

At about four o'clock, the reception doorbell rang. "I'll get it," I said, while I took a break from the document I was typing.

I opened the reception door to find Tony, the delivery driver from Archers, the company we use to buy all our stationery from. "Hi Tony." I smiled as I pushed the hair out of my eyes. "How's it going?"

"Not too bad darlin'," he grunted as he lifted a big box out of the back of the van. "Dunno what you've got inside this box, but it's bleedin' heavy."

"I think they're probably books. Val said she was expecting a delivery."

"Ah, that'll be it. I thought it might be something a bit more interesting, like bodies for research or something."

"Nothing as exciting as that I'm afraid." I chuckled. "But thanks anyway, Tony, you're a star."

"I think I've got an overactive imagination." Tony smiled as he jumped back in his van and went on his way.

I tried to lift the box Tony had taken off the back of the van, but it was far too heavy for me to pick up on my own, so I went inside the office and asked for Sasha's help.

She came out straight away. "Flipping 'eck, how many books are there in here?" Sasha asked when we lifted the box onto a pair of sack wheels. "Val never said, but probably quite a few 'cos she hasn't ordered any for ages."

I picked up the phone. "Val, I think the books you ordered have arrived. Tony has just delivered a great big box and it's really heavy, so I think it must be the books you ordered. Where do you want them?" I asked.

"Can you take them to the library and I'll unpack them in there and put them on the shelves."

"No problem. Me and Sasha put them onto some sack wheels so we'll take them down there now."

"Thanks a lot, that's really helpful," Val replied and put the phone down.

Sasha and I wheeled the box down to the library where we met Val already inside with her sleeves rolled up, ready for action. We used one side of a pair of scissors to cut open the box and took each book out, one by one, making a neat pile, ready for Val to put on the shelves. Each book had been carefully wrapped in bubble wrap, so we had sheets of the stuff in a pile on the floor once we'd finished unpacking.

"Thanks, girls. I'll take it from here," Val told us.

"We'll get rid of this bubble wrap for you," Sasha said with a sneaky look on her face as she scooped up the sheets ready to take down to our office.

We made our way back to our desks with sheets of bubble wrap in our arms.

"I know exactly what's going on in your head," I grinned as we started to lay out the bubble wrap on the floor. Once each piece was carefully placed over the carpet, we pulled our office chairs to one side and sat down.

"Ready?" grinned Sasha. And off we went. You could tell we'd done this before. We made a series of satisfying pops as we rolled our chairs this way and that over the carpet of bubble wrap. We continued to roll around until we were satisfied each bubble had been flattened.

I couldn't help but think that this should be offered on corporate away days. All of those bigwig companies that liked to splash their cash (or waste their cash, depending on how you looked at it) could be offered this as an option. A quick roll around the room on wheeled office chairs is so quick and easy and would cost a fraction of the price of a normal corporate activity.

"It's home time," I said. The day had gone so quickly it was hard to believe it was five o'clock already. Not needing much encouragement, we closed our computers down, put on our coats, shouted 'bye' to Val and left the office.

"See you tomorrow, babes," shouted Sasha as she walked the other way to me.

"Yeah, see you tomorrow," I replied to her retreating back. It had started to rain so I put my umbrella up just as a big gust of wind blew the umbrella inside out and ripped a big hole down one side. "I think I need a new brolly," I muttered to myself.

Chapter 2

$\mathcal{H}$ome for me was my one-bedroom flat, close to the centre of York. It wasn't classed as being in the city centre, that would have meant it was situated inside the bar walls. The city, or 'bar', walls of York are the most complete example of medieval city walls still standing in England today. Beneath the medieval stonework lie the remains of earlier walls dating as far back as the Roman period. That was enough history for one day.

I'd only been able to buy the flat with a large deposit using money that was left to me from my nan when she passed away. It had been nearly three years since she died, but I missed her every day. She was the kindest, gentlest and funniest lady you would ever care to meet. She had lost two husbands in her lifetime, the first of which had died in the Second World War. She'd rebuilt her life and got married for a second time and had a very happy and fulfilling second marriage until her husband, Jeff, died ten years ago. Her life experiences made her a wonderful source of information. Many times we'd talked late into the night as she'd shared her advice with love and care. I still have a lovely picture of her in a beautiful antique silver frame. It was taken during a long ago holiday to Skegness when she and Jeff had taken my brother and myself on holiday in a caravan. I can still remember the holiday, even though it was when I was about seven years old. It still makes me smile when I think of that holiday.

My flat was my little refuge from the world. It was the place that I felt warm, safe and cosy. It was only small, but was perfectly formed. I got a bit of noise from the neighbours every so often, loud music and shouting, but it was my little haven and I loved it.

On the walls, I had a collection of my own artwork. Most of the pictures were of people I knew, most of them going about their everyday life. I took random photographs on my phone and was able to reproduce the images using charcoal onto canvas, showing a true likeness of the person. Everyone who saw the pictures said I should become a professional artist or something using such talents. I never thought I was good enough. I've always had the memory in my head of my art teacher telling me that my, 'Pictures were good, but still lacking in emotion'. I can never forget her comments and believed ever since that my pictures were just OK, and certainly not good enough to pursue professionally. Sasha always told me to ignore the old bat, that that was one person's opinion and it was a pile of pants.

Of course, my family and friends were forever telling me that the pictures were stunning, but I've never had the courage to pursue a career in drawing. It seems a bit airy fairy, and at the end of the day, wouldn't pay my bills. It just seemed a dream too far away.

Just then the phone rang. I picked it up.

"Hello love," said the unmistakable voice in a strong Yorkshire accent. It was my mum.

"Hi, Mum, that was good timing, I've just this second walked in."

"Ha, ha, I told you I must be psychotic," Mum said gleefully.

"I think you must mean psychic, Mum." I smiled as I shrugged off my jacket.

"Yes, something like that love, you know what I mean."

That was one of mum's many foibles, she frequently got words muddled up which sometimes caused much hilarity in certain situations. Like, for example, the time when she was telling off some children who were throwing stones at a window. She was telling them that they should, 'Take some respinsibolty for their actions' but using the wrong word meant that the children sniggered under their breath, winding my mum up even further.

She also uses spoonerisms in her sentences, intentionally or not. In case you don't know what a spoonerism is, it's 'An error in speech in which corresponding consonants and vowels are switched between two words in a phrase'. For example, one of her favourite spoonerisms is to use 'par cark' instead of 'car park'. After she has watched the weather forecast she frequently informed me that, 'We are going to get some fist and mog', when she means mist and fog. There are many other spoonerisms that can be used which are really quite rude. I'm sure you can come up with some if you think long enough!

"I was just ringing to remind you about lunch on Sunday. Are you still coming?"

"Yes, I am. I wouldn't miss your roast potatoes for anything," I said as I stuck my head in the fridge looking for something I could have for my tea. Unfortunately, the full contents of my fridge included a small chunk of cheese, a yoghurt and an old onion. Even with my culinary skills I wouldn't be able to conjure anything up from that. I sighed. Either I could go to the supermarket and buy some food or I could get something from a takeaway. Takeaway food usually consisted of something rather greasy and fattening. I thought about trying to reduce my calorie intake by going and buying something healthy from the supermarket but supermarket shopping takes such a long time and a takeaway is very convenient. Takeaway it is then, I decided. I reached the fridge where all the menus for various takeaways were stuck on the door with magnets.

"Are Adam and Sarah coming on Sunday?"

"Yes, they both are. It will be good to see them because I haven't seen them for a few weeks now and I'm missing the catch-up."

Adam was my older brother by about three years. He used to make my life hell when I was growing up, taking every opportunity to try and get me in trouble. It never seemed to work though because my mum was wise to the fact. Now that Adam was older, he had certainly grown up and matured a bit. He still liked to tease me from time to time but it was all pretty harmless.

"You remember Tracey from number twenty-eight?" Mum asked. "Well she's getting married in September and asked me if you'd be free to do some pictures of the wedding reception. She said she'd pay you for them and wondered how much she would expect to pay?"

I had drawn some pictures for my friend taken at her wedding reception a couple of years ago. I had hidden myself away from all the action and took random photos of people, zooming in on their faces and catching them smiling or laughing, or sipping champagne from delicate glasses to toast the bride and groom. I caught those moments on camera and reproduced them on canvas. The result was a set of truly magical sketches of people caught in private moments, including a couple of the bride and groom gazing lovingly into each other's eyes. The pictures had done the rounds between friends and their families and I was being asked more and more frequently to do a similar thing at other people's wedding receptions. I loved doing this for people I knew, but at the moment it was purely limited to friends and family. I didn't have the heart to charge people for something that I enjoyed doing so much.

"Oh, if it's for Tracey I don't want to charge anything. I'll just take pleasure from watching her reactions to the sketches once they're finished."

"Yes, love, I told her that, but she still wants to pay you something. You could make a fortune doing this as a business, I keep telling you."

"Yes, Mum, I know lots of people who tell me I should set my own business, but it's such a big leap from regular employment to becoming your own boss, I'm scared. What if it doesn't work out and I don't earn enough to pay my bills? I don't think I'm good enough to work full-time drawing pictures. It just seems a bit of a pipedream of the moment."

"I know what you're saying, love, but you've got a real talent and you should use it to your advantage."

"Maybe one day," I said wistfully.

I finished the call with Mum telling her how much I was looking forward to lunch on Sunday. I decided I fancied a Chinese to eat and was able to order the Chinese quickly, due to the fact that (a) I knew the telephone number of the Chinese off by heart and (b) knowing exactly what the numbers for each dish were on the menu having ordered them so often before. After quickly ordering exactly what I wanted, I looked forward to my chicken chow mein, prawn toast and a pot of curry sauce on the side.

My takeaway came swiftly and I tucked in gleefully. Once I'd eaten it, I felt like a fat pig as I looked down at my bloated belly in dismay. "Was it really worth it?" I asked myself. "God, you bet it was! I'll worry about my belly later," I promised myself. I then spent the rest of the evening having a bath and shaving my legs, painting my toenails and plucking my eyebrows in preparation for the day shopping on Saturday with Sasha. After watching an evening of mainly reality TV, I got my PJs on, turned off the TV and settled down in my snuggly bed and fell straight to sleep.

Chapter 3

$\mathcal{T}$oday was Saturday. I love Saturdays. Saturdays meant two days off work to do whatever I like. Get up late, eat what I like (well, within reason), go shopping, go out drinking and getting ridiculously drunk.

I had arranged to meet Sasha after her driving lesson. We were going to meet up at a local pub for a spot of lunch and then go into town to buy lots of stuff for our holiday.

Sasha had been trying to pass her driving test for what seemed like years now. She had taken her driving test a total of seven times and each time she failed on what she said was a, 'Ridiculous minor fault'. In her eyes what was classed as a minor fault was in fact something quite serious like, for example, the time when she nearly ran over an old lady who was crossing the road at a zebra crossing who Sasha claimed, 'Was walking far too slowly and was there any wonder that I nearly hit her'.

I'd only ever been in the car with Sasha when she was driving on one occasion. And that one occasion was enough. They always say you should never teach a person to drive who is a close friend or relation and I can vouch for that. We ended up having a mega fallout and didn't speak for a week.

I was looking forward to my lunch, although I must admit that the Chinese I had last night seems to have upset my stomach a little bit. I think it will be a good idea to eat something light for lunch, see if I can settle my stomach. After all, we've got a full afternoon of clothes trying-on to look forward to.

I decided to walk to the pub because the weather was being kind for change. It was late April and spring was in full bloom, the trees drooping with the weight of blossom on their branches. There's nothing better than walking in the sun in springtime. I looked up towards the sky and felt the warmth of the sun on my face and felt an immediate happiness burst through me. I love this time of year. "Hello, Nan, I hope the weather is nice up there for you too." I often have little conversations with my nan. It's a way of feeling like she's still with me. I know she's not going to reply but I miss her every day and little comments to her make me feel much closer.

I walked into the pub at twelve thirty. I was spot-on time as I looked around the pub for Sasha. I knew she'd be somewhere near the bar. It was less distance to walk in between rounds.

Yes, I was right. She was parked right beside the bar.

"Hi Sash, how you doing?"

"I'm good thanks."

"How did the lesson go?"

"Yes, it went really well thanks. I've managed to get a cancellation for my driving test. It's only just over a week away. Clive thinks I should be well ready by then."

Sasha already had a little car just waiting for when she passed her test. It was only an old Mini, but Sasha loved it and couldn't wait to be able to drive it herself. To be fair, it has been sat waiting on the drive for a rather long time.

"Have you mastered your parking technique yet?"

"Yes, he made me practice parking literally a hundred times. I would say I managed to park successfully over half of those times." Sasha was prone to exaggerating somewhat.

"So, do you think you'll pass next time?"

"Oh God, I hope so. I can't bear it if I've got to go through it all again. That will be the eighth time I've taken my test."

Just then my stomach rumbled and made a loud growling sound.

"Wow, you sound like you're hungry," Sasha laughed. It appeared that my stomach rumblings were loud enough for other people to hear. "Quick, get a menu and let's order something."

Sasha grabbed a menu off the table and had a quick glance through it.

"What are you getting?" I asked, my stomach making some quite disturbing noises.

"I think I'll just get a sandwich and some chips. Yes, I'll have a chicken salad. In brown bread," Sasha decided.

"Well, I'll have the tuna sandwich," I decided. "And chips, of course."

"You stay there, I'll go order at the bar," I said, taking my purse with me to pay.

I reached the bar and saw that it was Dawn serving.

"Hi, Dawn, it's good to see you. I haven't seen you for ages."

"I know. It seems ages since I've seen you. I used to see you regularly with that guy, what's his name? Greg?"

"Nah, I haven't been in. And I haven't been with Greg for ages. The least said about that the better."

"Oh, I thought things were going really well with him?"

"Yes, so did I. Until I found out he was seeing somebody else behind my back."

"Oh God, what a dickhead. Well at least you found out sooner rather than later," grimaced Dawn while she stuck her hand inside a tea towel and dried and polished a pint glass.

"Yes, a lucky escape," I said, pulling a sad face.

I had been seeing Greg for about three months and I thought everything was going really well until Sasha was out in town with her boyfriend, Ben, and saw Greg kissing another girl. She felt really awful telling me that she'd seen him with somebody else, but I was glad that she told me. Plenty more fish in the sea and all that. Or so they say. I just wish I could find a king salmon instead of the minnows I seem to find myself with.

"All ordered," I told Sasha as I returned back to our table.

While we waited for our sandwiches, I took a quick selfie of me and Sasha grinning into the camera. It was a lovely photograph and I fully intended to make it into a picture.

"Is it hot in here?" I asked Sasha. "I'm really warm," I told her as I pulled my jumper off but suddenly realised I didn't have a T-shirt on underneath. I ended up just sat there in my tatty, grey bra while all of the pub seemed to turn to look at me. My cheeks reddened as I hastily put my jumper back on hoping that not many people had seen me.

I was mortified. I decided to keep my head down and hope nobody had spotted my cringeworthy striptease.

Just as I began to forget about the incident, I caught the eye of a young lad who was sat at the bar cradling his pint. He kept looking over at me with a smirk on his face. After five minutes of getting stared at, I decided to ask him what his problem was.

I looked over to him and asked, "Is there something behind me that you're looking at, or are you just looking at me?"

"No love, I was just wondering where you bought your underwear from?" he queried gleefully.

I couldn't be more embarrassed. He'd obviously seen me with my jumper off.

Turning back to Sasha, with my face aflame yet again, I chose to ignore him as we carried on chatting, mainly about what clothes and stuff we wanted to buy for our holiday.

"I'm dead excited already. It's only just over five weeks until we go away," Sasha exclaimed.

"I know, I've got the date circled on my calendar at home." I grinned. "In fact, it's forty-one days to go!"

I had been looking forward to this holiday for months, ever since we booked it in September last year. It was all paid for now, so we just had to look forward to the holiday which was fast approaching. We were lucky to be able to have the same week off work because it meant the office was really understaffed, but Val said, "We'll cope, just go for it."

Just then, Dawn arrived with our sandwiches.

"Wow, they look gorgeous," I said as my stomach made an ominous rumble again.

"I'll be back with your chips in a second," Dawn said as she placed the sandwiches on the table in front of us.

I took a big bite of my sandwich which was crammed full of tuna, red onion, sweetcorn and mayonnaise. It was delicious.

I looked over at Sasha and saw that she was doing her usual deconstruction process on her sandwich. She carefully removed the tomato and put it to one side. "I should have told Dawn that I don't like tomato but I forgot," she said whilst carefully placing the bread back on top of her sandwich again and taking a bite.

Sasha declared hers was equally as delicious and walloped it off in a matter of minutes. Although my sandwich was well nice, I could only eat half of it as my stomach began churning and bloating up, full of air.

"Are you OK, Rin?" asked Sasha with a concerned look on her face. "You've only eaten half of your lunch."

"Yes, I'm fine just not very hungry but my stomach has got really bloated. I look like I'm about to pop," I moaned as I pulled up my jumper and showed Sasha my belly.

"Oh my God, you look about six months pregnant!"

"Tell me about it. I've started to get really awful stomach pains too now. I think it's because I had some prawn toast for my tea last night and you know how sesame seeds affect me."

"Oh no," said Sasha. "If my memory serves me correctly you only get relief from bloating if you do a big fart."

"Yes, you're right and I think we need to go," I groaned as another griping pain shot through my insides.

Bearing that in mind, we made a quick escape and made a hasty retreat to the car park. I made a quick glance around the car park, making sure that nobody was in hearing distance and let rip, my backside making a noise that even Dumbo would have been proud of. Oh, bliss. I cannot begin to tell you how relieved I felt.

"Oh my God, I feel so much better now," I said.

"I bet you do, love. I'd have been proud of that one!" said a man's voice from above us. I looked up to see where the voice had come from and saw a man perched on the edge of the windowsill with the window wide open.

I could have died of embarrassment. Again. Sasha on the other hand found this exchange highly amusing and was bent double laughing, so much so, she was almost wetting herself.

"This really has to go down in our 'classic moments book'. Me and Sash kept a notebook in which we'd written down any funny things that had happened to us in the past. Things like the time I had had a bad cold and it was coming to an end, when the runny nose was drying up and instead was filled with thick green snot. I only realised how much I needed to blow my nose when one of the boys in our class cracked a joke and I laughed and a big green bubble of snot escaped from my nostril in front of the whole class. Or the time when Sasha walked out of the toilet in a nightclub with her skirt tucked into the back of her knickers and we didn't realise for about ten minutes and wondered why she was getting strange looks and sniggering in her direction.

We practically ran out of the car park, my cheeks aflame, whilst Sasha chortled away to herself.

We didn't have far to go until we were in the shopping centre of York and spent the next few hours trying on new outfits, sun hats, flip-flops and bikinis. We'd both bought tons of stuff and were truly knackered, but satisfied and happy with the things we'd bought.

I wriggled my fingers inside the handles of all of the carrier bags and repositioned them so they didn't dig in. There were so many of them it was only a couple of minutes before I had to readjust them again.

"I think it's time we went for a coffee somewhere, my feet are killing me," I suggested to Sasha.

"Yes, good idea. I need a wee as well."

"Let's go back to Marks. They do a lovely cream scone, and they've got good loos," I said as I readjusted my carrier bags once again.

We didn't have far to go back to Marks and Spencer's and we had no trouble finding a table. I think because it was quite late in the afternoon and the rush-hour had been and gone. I parked my bottom on a chair at a table and Sasha went off to get the drinks. And the cakes (the most important thing!).

She came back with a tray of goodies and it didn't take us long for us to eat our scones and have a slurp of tea.

"God, I needed that," I declared as I let out a quiet burp. Sasha wasn't as quiet as me and let out a much larger burp, sending heads flying round to see where the noise had come from. We sniggered to ourselves and picked up all of our carrier bags off the floor and made our way to the loos.

We shared a cubicle, as us ladies tend to do. I was in mid-flow when noises started to come from the cubicle next to us. It became obvious that whoever was in the toilet was having problems squeezing out a number two. The noises became louder and louder and me and Sasha tried to disguise our laughter and keep silent. Sasha was having trouble keeping her laughing quiet and she put her hand over her mouth in an effort to keep the noise in.

"Nnnnnnnnnggggggghhh," came from the next cubicle. And again another, "Aaaaaaarrrgh nnnnnnnggghhhhhh." Followed by what only can be described as a momentous splash as the offending log was jettisoned out at high speed.

By this time, Sasha and myself could no longer hold our laughter in and burst out of the cubicle and swiftly washed our hands. We were still drying them on paper towels when the cubicle door opened and a little old lady came out. She didn't look remotely embarrassed, almost as if she didn't think anyone else had heard her.

"Hello, girls," she said as she walked out of the toilet. She didn't even wash her hands. Euurguh.

"What is it today with the unfortunate bottom incidents?" Sasha asked as she threw the towel into the bin. She missed of course, so I bent down to pick it up.

"It's been eventful, you could say that!" I replied. "A day to remember, I think."

I kissed Sasha goodbye on the cheek and said I'd see her on Monday at work and then slowly walked back to my flat.

It would have been nice to have spent the evening trying on the things we'd bought on our shopping trip, but Sasha had a night planned with Ben, so I was home alone,

I took advantage of being home alone and took my phone out and brought up the photo I had taken of me and Sasha at lunchtime. It was a beautiful photo and was worthy of making it into a picture.

I set to work, and after only about twenty minutes, I had transformed the photo and made it into a picture. I was really pleased with the result and planned to show Sasha later and see what she thought.

My drawing things tidied away, I looked forward to a night of trashy TV. My only date was with a bottle of wine and the TV.

Chapter 4

I woke up on Sunday morning with a satisfied grin on my face, and once again looked through all of the things I'd bought yesterday on my shopping trip. Not long to go now! I thought happily to myself.

I was expected at my mum's at approximately one p.m. for dinner (or lunch depending on how posh you are). I didn't need to look smart for my mum so I pulled on a pair of jogging bottoms and an old jumper. It was important to have room for an expanding belly following one of my mum's Sunday dinners, so the tracky bottoms fitted the bill just fine.

I'd slept in quite late this morning so it was nearly midday by the time I slapped on a bit of make-up to make me look a little bit more presentable.

I felt a bit guilty that I hadn't done any housework for the past few weeks and the flat was looking a little bit grubby, so I vacuumed around quickly and washed up last night's dirty pots before putting a load of washing in the washing machine and setting the dial on a quick cycle. Good, that will be finished by the time I get back.

I grabbed my car keys from the side cabinet in the hallway, slamming the door behind me, making my way to the communal parking lot near my flat and climbed into Betty. Betty was my pride and joy, my little bit of independence I'd gained when I passed my test a couple of years ago. Having my own car and the ability to drive where I wanted, when I wanted, was the best feeling in the world. It's the point where you can truly begin to live your own life and not have to ask your mum and dad to take you here, there and everywhere.

I drove my way to mum and dad's house in Fulford just outside the centre of York. They had bought the house just after I'd started secondary school and had lived there ever since. I'd grown up in the house and had a fantastically happy childhood.

When I pulled up, I saw that Adam's car was already on the drive, a sporty little number by the looks of it. One I'd not seen before though. It will probably have cost a fortune. Adam and Sarah didn't have any kids so they were able to splash their cash on cars and holidays, so they were frequently away all over the world.

As soon as I got to the front door, I let myself in. I didn't need to knock as we treated it as if we still lived there. My bedroom was pretty much still the same as it was when I left and I sometimes found my way to my old bedroom to just reminisce.

"Hello, only me," I shouted as I walked into the hallway.

Mum came bustling out of the kitchen, apron on and looking rather hot and sweaty.

"Hello love, it's lovely to see you," she said as she bent forward for a kiss.

"Gosh, Mum, you're rather hot and slimy," I joked as I wiped the sweat off my cheek.

"Sorry, Erin but it is rather hot in here. All this effort adds up to a smashing dinner."

"Too right, I can't wait, I'm starving."

"Go in to the lounge, your dad, Adam and Sarah are in there. Dinner will be ready in ten minutes."

"Do you need me to do anything? Set the table, pour the drinks, get the mint sauce or horseradish out?" I asked, eager to help.

"Aye, you could put some horseradish in a bowl for me. I forgot to do that and we're having beef so we need a bit of horseradish," Mum replied, blowing some air up to her forehead to push her fringe off her face.

I got the horseradish sauce out of the cupboard and scooped a big dollop into a ramekin dish and added a spoon. I picked up the dish and set off to the lounge where I found everyone gathered around a brochure giving in-depth information about Adam's new car.

"I saw the new car on the drive, bro. It looks nice, what is it?"

"It's a Golf GTI, I've wanted one for years. It goes from nought to sixty in six point nine seconds, has a top speed of a hundred and forty-eight miles per hour and it's only got thirty-five thousand miles on the clock. Bargain."

"That's all well and good but where would you be travelling at a hundred and forty-eight miles an hour in it?" I queried.

"That's half the fun, just knowing that if I wanted to go that fast, I could."

"Well, as long as you're careful," I said as I looked over at Sarah. "What do you think of all this, Sarah? I thought you were happy with the old car?"

"Yes, I was well happy with it but when do my wishes come into it?" Sarah looked over at me with a resigned expression on her face.

"Well, you should put your foot down if you're really not happy. Adam will walk all over you if you let him."

"Yes, but you love it really Sarah. You're just as bad as me with all that posing you do with the music pumped up loud as you cruise the streets," said Adam with a big grin on his face.

Sarah rolled her eyes at me and we looked at each other and gave a knowing smile.

"Hi, Dad, how you keeping?"

"I'm good, all the better for seeing you. I haven't seen you for ages, you've been neglecting us."

"No, I haven't, Dad. I do have a hectic life you know. What with work, going out, partying, socialising, I just don't seem to get the time." I grinned.

41

"Yes, I guess you've got a life. We just don't see you as much these days," said Dad, the irony totally lost on him.

"I promise I'll make more of an effort to come and see you," I agreed.

Adam was still pouring over his car brochure when Mum came in with a plate of vegetables.

"I could do with some help bringing the other stuff in," Mum puffed as she placed the vegetables down on the table.

Adam and I went to carry in the rest of the bowls and plates from the kitchen and put them on the table.

"God, Mum, the smell is absolutely divine!" I smiled as I looked at the feast of food that we had placed on the table top.

"OK, everyone, sit down and get cracking. There's plenty more gravy if anybody wants some."

We helped ourselves to the feast of food before us. It was all cooked to perfection as usual, the meat slightly pink and melted in the mouth. The roast potatoes themselves were something to behold. I've never had nicer roasties in my life. Nowhere seemed to perfect the art of a truly magnificent roast potato like my mum. Just crispy enough on the outside yet still soft and fluffy in the middle and browned to perfection. I've tried to replicate my mum's roast potatoes, and although I made a mean roast potato, there was still something lacking.

The conversation went quiet. We all had our mouths too full of delicious food to speak. Once our belts and buttons began to strain under the mountains of food we'd eaten, we started to talk again.

"So did you have any thoughts as to whether or not you could do some pictures for Tracey's wedding?" Mum said picking a piece of meat from her teeth as she spoke.

"Oh, Mum, I'd forgotten all about it," I said.

"What's all this then?" asked Adam.

"Tracey from down the road has asked if our Erin will do some pictures of her wedding reception."

"I hope you said you do them, but at a cost," joined in Dad.

"Oh, Dad, don't you start. I said to Mum that I'd be more than happy to do them for free."

"Yeah, sis, you've got real talent there. You should charge for it. I know loads of people who would be prepared to pay hundreds of pounds for the service that you offer. I keep telling you, you should set up your own business, you would make a fortune," Adam declared, shortly after which he let out a rather large burp.

"Adam, that's gross," berated Mum as she frowned at him.

"I know, I know. I'm just too scared to take the leap. Why leave a secure job at the uni and set out on my own and risk not having enough money to pay my bills," I stated.

"Just to join in on the discussion, I know for a fact people at my work would love to use you for their wedding day. That time I took your pictures into the

43

office after you did June's daughter's wedding reception, the number of questions I had from people wanting to book such a service for their own kids' wedding, you'd have made a fortune," Sarah said.

"That is so nice to know, but I wouldn't know how to start a business. I'd have to think of a name to start with. Erin's Photos? Wedding Snaps 4 You? Erin's Picture Box? I just don't know where to start."

"So, should I tell Tracey you'll do it?" asked Mum.

"Yes, tell her I'll do it for fifty pounds," I replied.

"Fifty quid? You've got to be joking," laughed Adam. "It should be more like five hundred quid."

"No way, I couldn't charge five hundred pounds for something I enjoy doing," I stated.

"That's by the by whether you enjoy it or not. You should still charge for all your hard work. I agree with Adam, five hundred pounds sounds pretty reasonable for what you do," Dad agreed with Adam, nodding his head vigorously to get the point across.

"Yes, but five hundred pounds? That seems extortionate," I wriggled in my chair.

"I think that's cheap compared to the going rate. If you charge too little, people will think you're crap," Sarah argued.

"Yes, but just charge fifty pounds to Tracey. If I ever set up my own business, things will have to be different, I guess."

"Too right. Fifty quid, my arse. The quicker you get set up on your own the better." Adam declared.

"What's for pudding, Mum?" I asked hoping to change the subject and deflect any further queries from my family.

"Ooooh, I've got a lovely turd cart from the bakery down the road," said Mum. "I'll do some custard if anybody wants to have some with it."

"I think you mean curd tart, Mum," I laughed.

"Yes, that's what I said isn't it?" said Mum, completely oblivious to her error.

"Oh my God, Mum, that's brill!" chortled Adam.

And with that, Dad let out the biggest fart you've ever heard.

"Better out than in," Dad grinned, proud of his latest addition to the family discussion.

I rolled my eyes, feeling happy I was part of this crazy, mad family.

Chapter 5

*M*onday morning meant back to work. It was quite a busy week work wise because we had huggins of stuff to do. We barely had time to discuss our up and coming night out on Saturday but we were looking forward to a good night out. The only thing that was spoiling the anticipation, from Sasha's point of view, was her imminent driving test. During our lunch breaks (when we had time to have one) I asked Sasha lots of questions from the highway code book that she had clutched in her hand or on her desk.

"I don't know why I am so nervous this time," exclaimed Sasha.

"Maybe it means that this time you'll pass!" I replied as I concentrated on some complex figures that I was inputting in a report.

"Let's hope so," she said, whilst reading a section on road signs. All was quiet for a few minutes and then: "Oh, I can't be doing with this," wailed Sasha as she threw the book down on her desk in despair.

"I think you need to give it a rest for now. You can over think things and it makes it worse," I said as I leant down to pick the book up.

"Yes, you're right. I need to concentrate and finish this report off anyway," Sasha said with her business head back on.

It didn't stop me, however, from firing a barrage of elastic bands at her head in an effort to make her lighten up. Me and Sasha had constructed a huge ball made out of elastic bands wrapped around each other. That did the trick and it soon had Sasha grinning again.

Sasha and I had an aerobics class Thursday after work. We never wanted to go immediately before the lesson, but once we were in there, we got a little bit more enthusiastic. Only a little bit, though. As the end of the lesson got closer, we perked up a bit, knowing that soon we'd be in the pub. We probably drank more calories than we burned off in the lesson, but who cared. Every little helps, as stated by Tesco.

We found ourselves a table in the depths of the pub and Sasha got the first round in. I wasn't drinking alcohol, I was driving, and sat with my pint of lime and lemonade in front of me. It was quiz night on Thursday nights, which Sasha and I quite often found ourselves taking part in. We never won it, but we enjoyed getting a few questions right. That night it was packed. I was always on the lookout for potential boyfriends and as I scanned the room, my eyes fell on Greg, the bloke who'd cheated on me. Great, I thought, I could do without him being here. I decided the safest thing to do was just to keep my eyes down.

The quiz started and as the questions kept coming, I thought we were doing quite well. I had my head down, looking at our answers, when I became aware of somebody standing above me. I looked up to see Greg beaming down at me.

"Hi, babes."

"What do you want?" I asked him.

"I just wanted to say hello." And he just stood there. "And to say sorry for the way our relationship ended. It was stupid of me. I really regret what I did. I'm sorry," he wheedled.

I must say, my hackles were rising. "The only thing that was stupid was me thinking our relationship meant anything to you. Getting caught out ended up being a blessing in disguise. A lucky escape is how I see it," I fumed.

"I guess I'm wasting my time asking if you want to try again?" he asked.

I was flabbergasted. The barefaced cheek of the man.

"No. I. Do. Not. Want. To. Try. Again," I shouted at him. "Now I suggest you just turn around and piss off back to the stone you crawled from under." I couldn't make myself any clearer and Greg had the good grace to walk away with his head down.

"Way to go girlfriend. That was epic. You should have seen the look on his face!" Sasha said as she clapped her hands together.

"I feel so much better now, like I've had proper closure."

"He certainly hasn't been left in any doubt about where he stands with you now."

"Yes, I know. I also know we've missed the last three questions because of that dickhead."

"But it was worth it!" beamed Sasha.

We carried on answering the questions, but my heart wasn't in the quiz any more.

"Question thirty-seven," said Alan, the owner of the pub. "It's a 'guess the initials' question. OK, here goes... Which female tennis player with the initials GS was one of the leading players from the mid-1980s to the mid-1990s?"

"Ooooooooh, I know this, I know this," Sasha shouted.

"OK, who? Who is it, what should I put?" I asked her.

"Er, hang on a minute. Oh, I can't remember her name, you know, that woman."

"Yes, I know it's a woman, it said so in the question," I told her.

"Yes, you do know, it's that tennis player, the one with the hair". As all of the tennis players I knew had a full head of hair, I was still none the wiser. Sasha's face screwed up in concentration.

"Graffi Steph, GS… Graffi Steph," Sasha blurted out.

I frowned and then realised she got her letters mixed up. Steffi Graf is the name she meant. It was still the wrong answer, though. A few people snickered when they heard what she shouted.

"I think the answer's Gabriela Sabatini," said the man at the table next to us.

"Oh yes, Gabriela Sabatini, I meant," Sasha agreed.

"Oh, good grief," I said to myself.

Chapter 6

Sasha came round to my flat on Saturday afternoon, armed with all the paraphernalia we needed for a good girls' night out which included three different outfits and accessories for Sasha to wear. She didn't know which one to choose so had brought all three to try on and get my opinion.

"Flippin 'eck, Sash, you look like you're moving in!" I said as she struggled to carry the bags of stuff she'd brought.

"I must admit it was a bit of a struggle on the bus. It's not my fault I can't decide which outfit to wear."

Sasha promptly dumped the big pile of bags onto the sofa and flopped down.

"What I need is a drink, get the party started early!" she declared.

"I've got just the thing," I grinned making my way to the fridge in the kitchen. I opened the door and grabbed the cool bottle of prosecco I'd bought earlier, grabbed two glasses and took them into the lounge where Sasha was kicking off her boots and getting settled.

"Here's one I bought earlier!" I laughed as I unscrewed the lid from the bottle (none of the posh type that came with a cork!). "It is past three p.m. so I guess we're allowed to start the party early." I poured a generous amount into each glass and took a sip.

"That's lush," said Sasha as she took a gulp. And then another gulp. And another. Her glass was empty as she held it out ready for me to fill up.

I finished my own glass and topped each up from the bottle. It was more like drinking lemonade and we quickly polished off the lot.

"Here," I said to Sasha. "You know that selfie I took with my phone at the pub on Saturday last week?" I asked her.

"Yes, I remember it well. We both made ridiculously cheesy grins."

"Yes, that's the one. Well, I've made it into a picture to hang on my wall. What do you think?" I asked her while I held it up.

"OMG, that brilliant," exclaimed Sasha. "You've copied our grins perfectly, it's ace. Oh, Rin, you've got to do something about this. You're so talented, it's a crying shame that you haven't set up your own business yet," she stressed.

"Yes, I know, I know. You're not the only one who keeps telling me. But it's just too risky," I told her.

"But it's only risky if you might not have any work to do. But you've had loads of queries from people.

You'd be able to make a living from those queries alone."

"Yes, I know what you're saying. But I just can't take the risk."

"Risk my arse. You've just got to have faith in yourself girl!"

"OK, let's forget about that for now and concentrate on our night out. I think I'll go and get a bath and shave my legs," I said to a relaxed and settled Sasha.

"Yeah, babes, that's fine. I had a shower before I came round so I don't need one," Sasha said as she closed her eyes and laid back on the sofa. It only took a few seconds for Sasha to drift off to sleep so I took advantage of the quiet time to get my bath.

I filled the bath with hot water and added a generous squirt of bubble bath to it. I swirled the water around with my hand and built up a frothy mound of sweet smelling bubbles. I stripped off and lowered myself into the bath and laid there for a while just enjoying the warmth as I relaxed. After a while I got out my razor and shaved my legs and underarms. I didn't feel it was necessary to shave anything else, if you know what I mean, fat chance of anybody wanting to investigate that area tonight.

By the time I got out, dried myself and brushed my teeth, Sasha was up and about and had already put on the first outfit that she might wear and knocked on the bathroom door, opened it and stood there in the proposed outfit.

"What do you think? This is the first outfit of three potential ones. I was thinking perhaps this showed off a bit too much of my bottom," she said as she looked down to the floor, taking in her legs and trying to see how much of her bum was visible when she bent over.

"Hmmm, I see what you mean," I said as I stared at Sasha. "It'll be fine, as long as you never bend forward any more than a few inches."

"But I can't promise I won't bend over more than a few inches, especially after I've had a few!" Sasha stated. "I'll try on the next outfit and see what you think about that one," Sasha said, already wriggling out of the skirt that was about three inches wide from top to bottom (pardon the pun!).

The next outfit was just as revealing, but this time her boobs were on show. Even though she didn't have much on top, what she did have was that well pushed together and hoiked up that it didn't leave much to the imagination.

"Well, Sash, you certainly look very sexy and I'm sure you'd get the full attention of the boys if you wear that," I joked.

"Oh, but I love this top. At least the skirt is a bit more conservative," Sasha said, twirling around to see her reflection in the mirror. As it wasn't a very big mirror, she couldn't see much.

"What about the final outfit?" I asked hopefully.

"Just hang on a minute then, I'll go and try that one on," she said as she disappeared into the bedroom.

She'd only been gone a couple of minutes when she appeared at the door with the third outfit on. Although this outfit was perfectly acceptable, it just didn't look the sort of thing you'd wear on a Saturday night out, more for an interview.

"Well, that looks OK, but it's nothing exciting," I said.

"Well, I've tried all three on now, which do you prefer?" Sasha said with a frown on her face.

"I'd go for the second one. You may have half your chest hanging out, but at least you look like you're out for a good night," I commented.

"Yes, the second one it is then" agreed Sasha. "Put some music on, and let the evening commence!"

We spent the next three hours (yes, three hours — it takes time for a girl to get ready, you know) getting ourselves primped and primed, make-up put on and hair styled to within an inch of its life.

Finally, we were ready to go. Fortunately, because my flat was near the centre of town, we didn't need to get a taxi in and within a few minutes' walk, we were in the centre of the action.

First things first, we needed to eat and decided to try our favourite Italian restaurant, Giuseppe's. We were really fortunate and managed to get a table even though the place was heaving. I think it may also have been because of Sasha's cleavage helping matters because the maître d' was a young, hot blooded Italian who I'm sure appreciated the said appendage.

Stomachs full of food and already feeling a little bit squiffy, we started on the round of bars around the centre of York. We first made our way to Blinkers, where we pushed through the crowds of people and made our way to the bar.

"God, it's packed in here, I can hardly breathe," I said as I stood on my tiptoes trying to get the attention of the barman. It was also boiling hot. Once we'd been inside for a few minutes, we were absolutely sweltering. As I stood at the bar waiting to be served, I caught the eye of a rather attractive guy that was looking in my direction. Realising that he'd caught my attention, he gave me a cautious smile. I smiled back just as the barman walked over to me, and by the time I told him the drinks we wanted, the moment had passed and the guy had disappeared.

"Oh, fuck," I said in annoyance.

"What's up?" queried Sasha.

"I've just seen a really nice looking guy. We both flashed a smile at each other and then the barman came over and took my order for drinks and after that he'd gone. Just my luck."

"Don't worry, we'll have a good look around and see if we can find him," Sasha said pulling the top of her blouse closer together after her boobs looked like they were spilling out.

We searched the pub from one end to the other and couldn't find the guy. We finished our drinks and I realised that we weren't going to find him.

"I guess he's gone," I said and admitted defeat. "Come on, let's get to the next bar."

So we went to the next venue, and the next, and the next. I drank my drinks rather quickly because I was so disappointed that we couldn't find the guy. He could have been 'the one' and I'll never see him again.

By the time we decided to go to the club to have a bit of a boogie, my legs felt like they didn't belong to me and we wobbled our way to The Vibe, the city's favourite club at the moment.

Joining the queue to get in, Sasha was again the focus of attention, or should I say her cleavage was. After having far too many cocktails, I think Sash was oblivious to the fact and didn't care any more.

Finally, we made our way to the front of the queue, paid and made our way up the grand staircase, the music getting louder and louder the higher we reached. We pushed the main doors open and were hit with a heady mixture of heat and thumping music.

The beat was amazing, I could feel the music pulsing through my whole body and I found myself swaying in time to the rhythm of the music. I couldn't wait to get on the dance floor.

"Come on, let's go have a dance," I said as we made our way onto the dance floor. Soon we were strutting our stuff, losing all our cares and worries as we lost ourselves in the music. I love dancing, I feel completely relaxed and at ease, with no thoughts or worries to bother me. We danced for a while, arms in the air, punching and waving, dancing uninhibited to the tunes.

"Come on, I'm too hot. I need a drink," Sasha shouted as we made our way to the bar. As we squeezed through the crowds all eyes were on Sasha. She was stunningly gorgeous. She didn't really act as if she was God's gift to men, but she certainly was. The amazing thing was that she was totally unresponsive to any attention she got because her heart was purely with Ben, her boyfriend of three years. The love they had together was a beautiful thing. Every time I was in their company, I spent my time wishing that I could find someone who loved me, and I them, as much as Sasha and Ben did.

We found our way to the bar and I was amazed how quickly Sasha got served compared to me when I tried. No amount of squeezing my cleavage together and facing the barman with a full beaming smile helped me get served quicker. It certainly worked for Sasha.

Sasha turned from the bar and handed me my drink. "Thanks, I'm ready for this," I said as I took the glass from Sasha. I had no sooner taken a sip when I looked up and saw on my right the guy that had smiled at me in the bar earlier. He was deep in conversation with a man, but as the conversation ended and the man walked away, he glanced up and looked straight at me. Oh, flipping heck, caught red-handed. I quickly looked away and felt myself go red with embarrassment.

"Oh my God, it's him," I muttered under my breath.

"What's up with your shin?" queried Sasha, struggling to hear me over the music.

"No, it's him. The guy from the bar," I shouted.

"Brilliant, we found him!" Sasha grinned.

"Yes, and he's just seen me staring at him. So embarrassing."

"Is this him cos he's making his way over? This is so exciting!" Sasha asked excitedly.

Sure enough, he slowly walked over towards me. My stomach was churning as I swallowed. No matter how many times I got approached by a bloke, I was a nervous wreck.

"Hi, it was you I saw earlier in that bar, wasn't it?" he asked.

"Yes, it was me, for my sins." Oh man, I'd gone into stupid mode. Act cool Erin, calm down, I said to myself.

"I'm Trevor, and what's your name?"

"Erin," I said and gave him a nervous smile. "And this is my friend, Sasha." I nodded over at Sasha who was stood next to me wobbling from side to side, still under the influence of far too many drinks.

This was the point when men usually became fixated on Sasha and then chose to ignore me, but Trevor just said, "Hello", to her and turned back to me.

"Do you want to dance?" he said and took my hand and started dragging me towards the dance floor.

"Hang on, I need to get Sasha," I exclaimed as he continued to drag me off.

"Don't worry about me," Sasha yelled. "I've just seen an old friend from school, I'm going to go and have a catch up with her."

"OK, I'll see you later," I screamed at her whilst Trevor continued to drag me towards the dance floor.

Trevor held my hand all the way to the dance floor, just as one of my favourite tunes came on and I started to dance. This time, my dancing was rather more subdued than when I'd been dancing with Sasha. I didn't want to look an idiot, after all. Trevor started to dance, well, I say 'dance' but it was really more of the jiggle, he wasn't the best dancer I've known. Oh well.

We stayed on the dance floor for about ten minutes, after which Trevor said he needed a drink, so we left the floor and went over to the nearest bar.

"What do you want?" he asked.

"Bacardi and Coke, please," I replied.

We got our drinks and Trevor made his way to a nearby sofa where we sat down. I took a few tentative sips of my drink.

"So, what do you do for a living?" I asked him.

"I'm a mechanic at a garage near Osbaldwick. How about you?"

"I'm an administrator at the University of York," I said as I took another drink.

"Cool, how long have you been doing that for?"

"Oh, not long. Only about a year or so."

"Cool, where do you live? I live in Heslington, not far from where I work."

"I live in Layerthorpe, not far from the city centre."

"Cool, do you rent?"

Good grief, if he says 'cool' again I may have to slap him. "No, it's my place. I own it," I told him.

"Cool, you must be loaded!" he exclaimed.

"No, just fortunate, I guess. I used some inheritance money to pay the deposit on my flat. The mortgage still costs a fortune."

After that, the conversation became more stilted. We exchanged a few more pleasantries but it wasn't long before Trevor seemed more interested in kissing as he wrapped his arms around me and planted his lips on mine.

It had been ages since I'd kissed anyone, and I found the sensation quite pleasant. After a few minutes, though, Trevor poked his tongue inside my mouth and started doing weird circling motions. I guess he thought it was quite nice, but it actually made me feel quite nauseous. I'd like to think it was the kissing that was making my head spin, but I think it was more likely due to the large quantity of alcohol I'd had.

"Are you all right?" Trevor queried as he looked at me with concern.

"Yes, I'm fine, just a little bit hot."

"Do you want to get out of here?" he queried.

"Yes, I think I've have had enough now," I replied as I turned my head this way and that looking out the Sasha. "I don't know where Sasha is though," I cried. It was always a rule between me and Sasha that we always stuck together on our nights out and didn't leave without the other. There was no way I was going to leave without Sasha now.

Just at that moment I spotted Sash and waved over to her. Sasha quickly said her goodbyes to her friend and made her way over to Trevor and me.

"I've had enough now and I'm ready for home, I don't know about you?" I asked Sasha, hoping she was ready to leave.

"Yeah, let's go home now. It's been a good night but I've still got to revise tomorrow for my driving test on Tuesday," stated Sasha. "I'll go out and flag down a couple of taxis."

"Are you going straight home, babe? You could always come back to my place," Trevor said optimistically.

"No, it's home time for me now." I pulled a face, hoping that Trevor would understand, besides which, there was no way I was going to go any further with him the first night I'd met him.

"What if I came home with you? Carry on where we left off."

I just looked at him and raised my eyebrows. I think he got the message.

"Oh well, it's been nice meeting you anyway," he said with a resigned look on his face. "Maybe we could go out some time?"

"Oh, ah, erm, yes OK that would be good. I tell you what, why don't you come out with me, Sasha and Ben, her boyfriend, sometime next week?"

"Yes, OK, that would be good. Give me your phone number and I'll ring you tomorrow," he said passing me his phone. I typed my number in and passed it back.

"Thanks, that's great," he said as he leant in for a kiss. This time, I didn't let it linger and pulled quickly away.

"OK, speak to you tomorrow then."

"Yes, speak to you then." And with that he disappeared back into the club.

"I'm sorry I landed you and Ben in it and said we'd go out with him next week, but I'm not sure how I feel about Trevor just yet and maybe a night out will make it a bit clearer in my head," I explained.

"No worries, let's see if he does ring tomorrow and then we'll have to think of where to go, probably somewhere for a bar meal or something," Sasha agreed.

"Thanks, Sash, I knew you'd understand." I smiled and let out a big yawn. I was ready for my bed. We stood in the queue for taxis for about ten minutes. The taxi pulled up and we both climbed in, stopping first at Sasha's house, then my flat.

My bed was waiting for me. Bliss. At least this time I managed to keep both heels on my shoes!

Chapter 7

I woke up on Sunday morning (well, I say morning, but I only just made it at 11.57 a.m.) feeling a little worse for wear. I looked at myself in the bedroom mirror. One quick glance was all it took to realise that I shouldn't have bothered looking at my reflection and should stay well away from mirrors for the time being.

I thought back to last night with Sasha. It was a brilliant night, I really enjoyed it. My stomach lurched when I thought about the evening's events with Trevor. I haven't quite worked out how I felt about Trevor yet. He seemed like a really nice guy, but there was something about him I couldn't quite put my finger on. I barely knew him. Anyway, he said he was going to ring me at some point today, but I haven't had a phone call yet I thought as I checked my phone for messages and missed calls.

I decided I needed to give my place a good clean. I set about dusting and polishing all the surfaces and putting all my clothes into the wash. I didn't stop until the washing basket was empty and all of the surfaces were gleaming. I put the latest Little Mix album on the radio, pumping the music up to full volume and I danced around like a maniac while I vacuumed the carpets. All the while I kept checking my phone to make sure Trevor hadn't called. There was nothing from him and I had almost given up hope of receiving anything. "Oh well, so be it," I said to myself whilst I put the Hoover away. Just then the phone rang.

My heart skipped a beat. If it was Trevor, I didn't want to answer the phone too quickly and make out I was too keen, but then again, if I didn't answer it fairly quickly, he might ring off and I'd never hear from him again. How I hated these 'what ifs' in a new relationship. I just wanted to feel completely at ease and relaxed and not have to wonder if I was playing it correctly.

"Hello," I said as I picked up the phone.

"Hello, babes it's me," said a voice at the end of the line.

"Me?" I replied, trying to play cool.

"Me, Trevor, from last night," muttered Trevor, in a much less confident tone.

"Oh, hi. Sorry I didn't recognise your voice."

"I said I was going to ring you, don't you remember?"

"Of course, I remember, I'm only joking."

"Oh, OK, that's all right then. Are you still up for going out next week?" Trevor asked.

"Yes, that will be fine. Shall we say Tuesday night?"

"Oh, I can't do Tuesday, I play football with the lads on Tuesday night."

"Thursday?"

"Yes, I can do Thursday."

"Yeah, I'll have to check with Sasha and Ben that they can make Thursday night, but if you don't hear from me, Thursday night will be fine. I'll pick you up at seven thirty," I agreed.

"Right then, it's a date. Where are we going?" asked Trevor.

"I'll book a table at a pub near my flat. Oh yes, I'll need your address won't I," I remembered.

He quickly reeled off his full address.

"OK, I'll see you on Thursday, seven thirty p.m.," he said. I could almost see the smile on his face from his voice.

"See you Thursday," I replied and put the phone down. I felt well excited for Thursday but also a little apprehensive. I didn't know what to wear for starters. Oh well, I'll worry about that later. I needed to ring Sash to check if her and Ben could make it on Thursday night.

I picked up the phone and dialled Sasha's number. She answered it on the third ring.

"Oh hi, Rin," she answered. "I'm having an awful day. Ben has just been testing me on the highway code and I keep getting every question wrong. I can't get the speed limits right and every road sign that Ben holds up to ask me what it means, I get wrong. Ben has taken me out driving and I keep doing all of the manoeuvres wrong, I can't park for toffee and my reversing round a corner is a disaster," cried Sasha.

"Oh Sasha, calm down. You're overthinking things. You need to step away from the highway code book and just chill," I suggested. "Go out for lunch, have a few drinks and relax. Your driving test isn't until Tuesday. You've done enough preparation now. Just a quick flick through the highway code an hour before your test should be enough. Don't overthink things and you'll be fine," I said with my sensible head on.

"Yes, OK, you're right. I wish I could be as calm as you."

"Yes, but I'm not always as calm. Anyway, on a different note, Trevor phoned and we agreed to go out for something to eat on Thursday night at seven thirty. Is that OK with you?" I asked.

"Is Thursday night OK for you to go out with Erin and Trevor?" I could hear her asking Ben.

"Yeah, Thursday night will be fine," said Ben from across the room.

"Yes, Thursday will be fine for both of us. Shall I book a table?"

"No, that's OK. I'll book a table at the Golden Oak."

"Mmmmm, the food is lush there. I'm looking forward to it already."

"Yeah, me too. I'll go and book it now. I'll see you at work tomorrow but in the meantime please just relax."

"Yeah, I'll try to relax, see you tomorrow," Sasha replied as she rang off.

Chapter 8

"*O*h, God," Sasha moaned, with her head in her hands. "I'm never going to pass, I'm destined never to pass my driving test, I should just accept it."

"Don't be such a defeatist," I argued. "You're going to be fine, just calm down."

It was Sasha's driving test in just over an hour and she was bricking it, to put it mildly. She always got like this before her test, so it was nothing new. "You'll be fine once you get sat behind the wheel," I pointed out.

"I know, I know, I've been there so many times before and it's always ended up a disaster. I'd better get going otherwise I'm not going to be there on time."

"Yes, I hope everything works out fine, I have every confidence in your increased abilities," I grinned.

"OK, I'll be back later. Fingers crossed," Sasha said hopefully as she left the office and crossed over the road to where Clive, her instructor, was waiting.

"I do hope she passes this time. I don't think I can cope with this for much longer, and I'm sure Sasha can't either." Val spoke quietly from the office doorway.

"I have every confidence in her," I stated sarcastically. "Maybe some people are destined never to pass their driving test, Sasha being one of them. She's not the best driver in the world, bless her."

The next couple of hours flew by as I got my head into typing a report for one of the researchers at the centre. It followed the results of a long study into people's quality of life when they've got cancer. It sounded quite harrowing, but I found it very interesting.

I looked up when I heard somebody open the office door. It was Sasha, with a sullen look on her face.

"Oh my, your face says it all. It didn't go well again I take it?" I queried.

"No, no, no. It didn't go well," croaked Sasha.

Here we go again, another fail.

"It went... brilliantly well. I've only bloody well gone and done it. I passed! I can't believe it!" Sasha said with the biggest grin I've ever seen on her face, even bigger than when she won two hundred pounds on a scratch card!

"Oh my God, I don't believe it. I mean, yes, I do believe it. I'm so chuffed for you, you must be ecstatic!" I beamed.

"Yes, I can't believe it either. No more lessons on Saturday mornings, no more revising, no more practising and no more Clive." Sasha smiled.

"Yes, no more Clive. He's had to put up with you for such a long time. I bet he's more relieved than you are."

"I told Ben I passed my test and he was so pleased for me. He did point out that I can drive on Thursday night now when we go out with you and Trevor."

"Absolutely, but you do realise that you won't be able to drink?" I pointed out.

"I know, but it'll be worth it. I can't wait to go out in the car on my own."

"When you've passed your test and you go out driving on your own, that's when you really start to learn to drive properly. Remember when I turned around that corner too quickly and scuffed all the side of my car on that van. That was two days after I had passed my driving test. When I look back on it now, I really had a lot to learn about driving," I stated with my serious head on. Oh my gosh, I'm turning into my mother!

"Yes, but you're really good at driving now. I just hope I can get to be as good as you."

"Wow, thanks babe. That really makes me feel good," I replied, my chest puffing out as I took on board the compliment.

Just then Val appeared at the door, carrying a big cake with a lit candle in it. "I had every faith in you, congratulations," gushed Val with the big smile on her face.

"Aw, is that for me?"

"Well, I don't see anyone else around here with something to celebrate."

Sasha approached the cake and with one quick puff, blew out the candle.

Val cut the cake into six even pieces and handed out a piece to everybody there, managing to drop a big dollop of icing on the floor. Val reached down quickly and scooped up the icing before somebody slipped on it.

I took a quick photo of Sasha with her mouth wide open just about to bite a humongously large piece of cake. "Mmmm, that's well nice," mumbled Sasha while her mouth was full. I could hardly hear what she was saying, but I got the gist. "Thanks Val, you're a star," Sasha managed to say before she took another bite of cake.

"Yes, well you deserve it," Val replied. "But as soon as you finish that cake, you need to get on with work. Ken has still got a report that he needs typing."

To me, Val said in a stage whisper, "At least I've finally managed to get to use the candle. I've been holding on to it for the past three years!"

"Sure thing, boss. Right on with it," Sasha agreed as she finished off the last piece of cake on her plate.

"I need to get work finished ASAP so that I can go out and drive. Watch out roads, here I come!"

God help us, I couldn't help but think. I know Sasha deserves to have passed her test, but you wouldn't call her a confident and good driver. Those words just did not spring to mind when you thought about Sasha behind the wheel. Oh well, like I said earlier, once you've passed your test, the learning really begins.

Chapter 9

*T*hursday night came around all too quickly. I was really nervous about my impending evening with Trevor. I phoned Sasha to check she was still up for the evening.

Once I got through to Sasha on the phone, she filled me in with all her trips in her car and how well she had driven on her own. "It's really weird not having somebody sat next to you in the car. I found it quite daunting at first, but now I love it, putting the radio on, winding down the window and letting the wind blow through my hair."

"Go steady though, don't get too cocky," I said as I tried to impart some advice.

"God, don't be so miserable. I'm enjoying my independence, it's great," she pointed out. "So, what are you wearing tonight?" asked Sasha. I could tell she was blowing bubbles while she spoke. I could hear her champing and the occasional pop. Sasha loved bubble-gum. She always had a stash of different flavours in her bag. Her favourite was Anglo bubbly that she used to buy when we were at junior school together. She had discovered, to her delight, that she could still buy them during one of her searches on retro sweet shops. She also had a liking for golf balls. No, not the ones you play a game with hitting the ball around a golf course, no I mean the bubbly ones that were white and round, like gobstoppers, with lots of little bumps on the surface and were quite hard to chew.

"I don't think I'll wear anything fancy, just jeans and a top, I think. We are only going to the Golden Oak for a pub meal after all," I stated as Sasha popped another bubble down the phone.

"I think I'll wear that new top I bought from Marks the other week, you know, the one with the pink hem."

"Yeah, I love that top. If they'd have had it in my size, I'd have bought one too. The lady said they only did it up to a size sixteen. I might've just squeezed into it, but I'd have been uncomfortable all night."

"Like when you bought that size sixteen jumper and they didn't have any smaller sizes. I love that jumper. You can't win them all." Sasha popped.

Just at that point, I heard Ben calling Sasha in the background. "OK, babes, got to go. Me and Ben are going to choose some wallpaper for the spare bedroom. It's usually quite easy to choose because we both have the same tastes. Anyway, I'll see you tonight at about seven o'clock in my car. It'll be the first time you've been in my car since I passed my test. You'll be able to tell me if my driving is any better than the last time you were in the car with me. Have you got Trevor's address?" Sasha asked.

"Yes, I've got it. He lives not too far from the Crown so he won't have to put up with your driving for too long," I said, laughing.

"Oy, you, cheeky mare."

"Can't wait, I'll see you about seven," I said and hung up the phone.

I started sorting through the pictures in my portfolio. There were a lot of old sketches I'd drawn over the years, some of them I'd made at weddings, some were of my friends. I placed some of the sketches to one side, putting the better ones back into my portfolio.

Next, I opened the camera app on my phone and searched for the picture of Sasha I'd taken at work when we had the cake to celebrate her passing her driving test. As I scrolled through the photos, I found the one I was looking for. It was the one where Sasha was taking a huge bite of the cake. I loved it, and it caught the moment beautifully. I'm sure Sasha wouldn't think much of it, but I took some drawing paper out of my file and started copying the photograph with charcoal. I smudged and blended the black edges and worked on her face and its expression. I drew the fallen strands of her hair which fell across her face, the shape of her cheeks and the arc of her neck. It was a face I knew so well.

I worked non-stop on the picture for about an hour. I held the finished image up and took a critical gaze at it. I was quite pleased with the result. I wasn't sure Sasha would be as equally pleased, but I'll show her it and see what she thinks.

I tidied the paper and charcoal neatly away, shoving the portfolio back under the sofa out of the way. It was only something that I shared between family and friends and would stay under the sofa until next time I worked on it.

By the time I finished with my drawing, there wasn't much time left for me to get ready for my night out. For that, I was grateful, because it meant I didn't have to worry for hours before going out. I had pretty much decided what I was going to wear and took the shirt and jeans out of my wardrobe and placed them on my bed. I quickly took a shower, washed my hair and got dressed. I was quite pleased with my choice of outfit. Not too dressy and not too casual. The Golden Oak wasn't somewhere where you needed to get dressed up for.

A quick spray of perfume and a lick of lip gloss and I was ready. I sat casually on the sofa with a small glass of wine while I waited for Sasha to come and pick me up. While I sat, I let my emotions get the better me and started worrying about how the night will progress with Trevor. Would he like what I was wearing? Am I dressed too casually? Have I got something stuck

75

between my teeth? Have I got garlic breath? Flippin 'eck, Sasha, hurry up.

As my thoughts continued to worry me, I heard a car horn beep outside. I pulled the curtains back a little bit and peered out. Sure enough, there was Sasha in her little car. I rushed out of the door and locked it behind me, hanging the straps of my handbag across my shoulder.

"You're dead on time," I said as I climbed onto the back seat of the car.

"I know, but that's probably because we set off about half an hour ago. I had to stop and get some cash out of the hole in the wall," Sasha laughed.

"Hi, Ben," I said as I strapped my seat belt on. "I hope Sasha's driving hasn't made you feel sick before we eat!"

"Hi, Rin. We drove here quite safely with very few incidents. I would imagine the little old lady we nearly ran over would beg to differ!"

"Oy, you. There was no such little old lady. If I wasn't driving the car, I'd give you a shove."

"Only joking, love. You know I'm only kidding," Ben said.

"What's Trevor's address then?" asked Sasha.

"It's not far from here, just off Hull Road. I've never been myself, but just put his address on the satnav, we should find it fine."

"Satnav. What satnav? This car doesn't have such technological delights, it's way too old!" Sasha informed me. "Just give Ben the address and we'll go from there."

"OK, it's number twenty-four Lilac Avenue."

"You're in luck, I have a mate who lives down that road. I know exactly where it is," Ben piped up.

It was only a short drive to Lilac Avenue from my flat so we were there in ten minutes. "This is it," I shouted as I ran my fingers through my hair and fluffed it up a bit. I rolled my tongue over my teeth to try and get my mouth to work properly. I was feeling very nervous indeed as Ben beeped the car horn to signal we were there.

Within seconds Trevor appeared at the door with a big grin on his face. I could see he had made an effort for the occasion as he was wearing a shirt and tie. That would look fine in the right setting, like for an interview or something, but not really in the Golden Oak.

Trevor made his way over to the car door and opened it and stepped in. We were greeted by an overpowering blast of Aramis aftershave. It was so strong my eyebrows started to sizzle.

"Hi, babe. Are you OK?" Trevor whispered.

"Yeah, I'm fine. You've met Sasha, and this is Ben." I indicated with a nod of my head.

"Hiya, mate. Nice to meet you."

With the introductions complete, we drove to the Golden Oak and managed to get a space in the already overcrowded car park. The only conversation that had taken place was between Sasha and Ben. Trevor and myself sat in silence at the back, while Trevor thought it best to rest a hand on my thigh and squeeze it. The aftershave was really overpowering and was starting to give me a headache and make me feel quite sick.

We all climbed out of the car and made our way to the entrance of the pub.

"What does everyone want to drink?" asked Ben as we approached the bar.

"I'll have a glass of white wine, please," I replied.

"I'll just have a diet coke," smiled Sasha. "Seeing as I'm driving." The novelty of being designated driver was still new to Sasha, so she didn't mind not having a drink. Let's see how she feels in six months' time.

"I'll have a pint of Theakstons, if that's OK," asked Trevor. "Where are the menus? I'm fucking starving."

I was a bit taken aback by the language he had used. I glanced over at Sasha and raised my eyebrows.

"Hello, have you got a table booked?" came a voice from behind us. We all turned round in unison and looked to see a small girl, not much older than about sixteen, pleasantly dressed and with the big smile on her face.

"Yes, we've got a table booked for eight p.m. in the name of Cooper," I replied. The girl glanced down to a clipboard she had in her hands.

"Ah yes, I see it. Follow me. I'll take you to your table, it's ready."

The girl showed us to our table which was neatly decorated with a small vase of flowers in the centre next to an array of glasses to suit everybody's choice of drinks: wine glasses, water glasses and champagne glasses.

"Oh my God, this is a bit poncey isn't it," remarked Trevor as he struggled to find a space for his pint of beer.

"Well, I think it's lovely," retaliated Sasha as we all sat down.

The waitress then passed a menu to each of us and we quickly had a look at what was tonight's choices.

"Wow, it's a bit pricey. I was hoping it was going to be chicken in a basket for a tenner," joked Trevor. Well, I was hoping he was joking, but I don't think he was.

"Me and Sasha have eaten here loads of times before. The food might be a little bit more money, but the meals are worth it," commented Ben.

"I think I'll have a steak. I haven't had a steak for ages," Trevor decided. "And prawn cocktail to start with."

We all carried on looking at the menus and decided what we were going to eat. Not long after, the pretty waitress came and took our order. She took our menus away and walked back towards the kitchen.

"Look at the arse on that," Trevor commented as she walked away. "I wouldn't mind giving her one."

Me, Sasha and Ben looked uncomfortable. I was appalled that Trevor had made comments like that. Who says things like that when you're with a potential girlfriend? And you don't say things like that in front of a couple you've never met before. I squirmed with embarrassment.

The food arrived and we dug in. It was delicious and the conversation went quiet while we ate our meals, not because our mouths were full, no, it was more because we didn't know what to say and the conversation dried up.

Ten minutes later and our plates were empty, the meals thoroughly enjoyed by all. My jeans were feeling rather tight. I didn't think I could fit a dessert in. It might be the ending of me! Trevor sat there trying to pick meat out of his teeth, not discreetly, but making it blatantly obvious that he was struggling.

"Do you want me to ask if they have any toothpicks?" I asked him. "It looks a bit embarrassing with your fist practically in your mouth."

"No, babe, it's all right I've got it out now, look," he said and proceeded to stick his finger in my face, on which sat a sad looking bit of gristly beef. Right at that moment Trevor decided to emit a thunderous burp. I couldn't help but notice the diners on tables close by turned round to see where the noise had come from.

"Oops, sorry about that," Trevor grinned, not looking the least bit sorry.

"Shall I get the bill?" I asked Sasha and Ben. They could both tell I'd had enough of the evening, and Trevor.

"Yes, good idea," replied Sasha.

"Are we just going to divide the bill into four?" asked Trevor. There wasn't even an offer for him to pay for my part of the meal. I wouldn't have expected him to, but it would have been nice to be asked.

"Yes, OK, whatever," Sasha replied.

We asked for the bill, and paid the waitress when she arrived. We couldn't wait to get out to the car and get home. It seemed that Trevor felt a little differently as to how the evening had progressed. "Shall I come in for a coffee then?" he asked me.

"I don't think so, no."

"Oh well, your loss," Trevor responded.

Trevor was the first one to be dropped off at his house and when he walked up the path he didn't look back.

"Oh my God. Good riddance is what I say," I commented as a watched his back disappearing inside the front door.

"I can't believe it. What a male chauvinist pig. I think that's the last we'll see of him!" Sasha snorted.

"Too right, what a loser. What was going on with their aftershave anyway? It was so strong it was making my eyes water."

"And what the hell was he wearing? He looked like he was going for an interview with that shirt and tie on. And that tie was grim, it looked like something my grandad would wear to a funeral."

"OK, OK, I get the message. He was a loser. Again," I mumbled.

It was only a quick drive to my flat. I kept my head down and didn't speak, my mind replaying some of the evening's awful incidents. Within minutes, Sasha pulled up alongside my flat.

"Aww, babe. I'm sorry he turned out to be a wanker. You'll meet someone soon, someone special, you'll see," Sasha insisted. I wasn't too sure I shared Sasha's optimism.

I gave Sasha a quick peck on the cheek. "Thank you. I'll see you at work on Monday, Sash," I said as I closed the door behind me and walked slowly to the front door. Once inside, I made my way to my bedroom and threw myself dejectedly onto my bed.

I felt very sorry for myself. I let the tears fall. When would I ever find someone decent? I'm not a bad person, didn't I deserve someone special?

Chapter 10

With all thoughts of Trevor put behind me, I started work on Monday morning with a more positive attitude. It was only four weeks until we went on our holiday. I was getting more and more excited.

I got into the office and set about making my way through the pile of letters and reports that needed attention.

I was miles away when Val put her head round the door and asked, "Where's Sasha? She hasn't got an appointment at the dentist or doctor or something and I've forgotten?"

"No, nothing. That's weird, she's usually on time for everything." I frowned. "I'll give her a ring and see where she is."

I rootled around in my bag looking for my phone. It was right at the bottom, as usual. I dialled Sasha's mobile number and it went immediately to answer phone. Sasha hardly ever put her phone on answer phone. "Hi Sash, it's me. Just wondered where you were. Give us a ring when you get this message."

"She's probably trying to park her car. You know what the car parks are like on campus. Nightmare."

I carried on working, but I had an uneasy feeling in my stomach that I couldn't quite seem to shift. I dialled her number a few more times, but each time I just got the message: *The person you are calling is unable to take your call right now, please leave a message after the beep.* It was almost lunchtime and I still hadn't heard from her. I was getting really worried now. What the hell was going on?

I decided to call Ben, I'm sure I had his number. I scrolled through all of the contacts on my phone and found him. I dialled his number straight away. Again, the same as Sasha's phone, it went straight to voicemail and asked me to leave a message. "Hi, Ben, it's me, Erin. Sasha hasn't turned up for work and I can't get hold of her. She's not answering her phone. I'm sure it's nothing, but do you know where Sasha is? It's not like her to not turn up for work without a valid reason. If you know where she is, can you ring me and let me know. I'm sorry if I'm fussing, but well, it's just not like Sasha to be in late…" And with that, someone answered the phone. Nobody said anything. I could tell there was someone there though. "Hello, Ben, is that you?" The phone stayed silent. "Ben? Ben?" Again, there was just silence. "Ben is that you? Please speak, you're scaring me".

I heard a faint sniff. Silence again. Then a voice came down the phone. It was Ben's voice, but it sounded strange. "Erin, I…" Ben croaked.

"What is it, what's happened?" I could tell there was something very wrong, I was scared to ask, but I had to know. "Ben, has something happened to Sasha? Ben… Ben?"

"Oh, Rin. Something awful has happened. Sasha … she car drive to work. She took the car." Ben wasn't making any sense, his sentences were not forming correctly.

"She drove to work? Is that what you're trying to say?" I pleaded.

Ben started sobbing down the phone. I've never heard a man cry before. I wanted to reach out and touch him, wrap my arms around him, but I needed to know everything, all of it.

My hand gripped my phone. "Ben, Ben, what's happened? Please tell me, is Sasha all right?"

I could hear Ben sniffing, then his voice came back on the line, this time stronger and more in control but what he was telling me, I didn't want to know.

"…She hit another car coming round the corner head on and she… and she… didn't stand a chance."

"What do you mean, she didn't stand a chance? Where is she? Is she in hospital? How badly hurt is she? Can I go and see her?"

Now Ben was really crying, uncontrollable sobs down the phone, like an injured animal. I could tell there were people around me, aware that something was going on. They huddled around my desk, concerned looks on their faces as they tried to make sense of the horror unfolding.

"Ben, is she in York District Hospital? Why aren't you there? Can I go and see her?"

Ben was almost incoherent down the phone as I tried to listen to what he was saying.

"Noooooo. She's dead... died. They... to help, but the car was a mangled... even get her out of it... Dead. Sasha... dead."

"No, no, no," I heard myself saying, over and over again, as I realised what Ben was trying to tell me. My legs gave way and I landed on the floor. "Not Sash, no, no, no," I repeated to myself and I let out a scream and everything went black.

Chapter 11

I was sitting on the edge of my bed with the intention of getting dressed, but I just couldn't be bothered. I couldn't be bothered with anything.

It was a week now since Sasha had died. A week since I'd last spoken to my best friend. A week since I'd heard her dirty laugh. A week since I'd seen her beautiful face. A week since I'd held her hand. A week since I'd shared a joke with her. A week.

When some people describe death, they say someone has 'passed'. Passed where exactly? Straight down the road and next left at the traffic lights perhaps? The phrase seemed too trivial, too gentle, almost pleasurable. It didn't tell you about the aching pain that grief envelops you in. It doesn't prepare you for the gaping hole that's left in your heart.

No, as far as I'm concerned, my best friend had died. She is no more. It was as simple as that.

A week was hardly any time, yet it felt like a lifetime. I was unable to dig myself out of this dark place, this place that had me consumed with an overwhelming sadness that lived with me every minute of every day.

I've tried to claw my way out of this torment. I don't feel like I deserve to be here, like it should have been me that was killed, not Sasha. Those negative thoughts never helped anybody. It wouldn't bring Sasha back.

I had tried to eat something, to drink something but I can't seem to keep anything down, my stomach rejecting anything I put into it.

I keep catching the smell of my unclean body. I haven't had a shower for days. My armpits stink and my hair is lank and greasy. It's been a week and I can tell I've lost weight.

Mum keeps calling me to check how I'm doing. The conversations are painfully slow with one-word answers from me. I'm getting better though, I'm managing to speak whole sentences now. I can tell she's suffering as much I am. After all, Sasha was like another daughter to her, but she's dealing with it better than I am. She'd known Sasha since she was a little girl. She'd spent days around our house, enjoyed day trips and holidays with us and my mum missed her just as much as I did, well, not quite as much may be?

The phone rang, probably Mum checking up on me. She hadn't called since yesterday teatime, so it was about time I had my regular check-in.

"Hello love, it's only me, Mum." She always said the same thing, as if I didn't realise it was her when I heard her voice.

"Hi, Mum"

"How are you doing? Peggy was asking after you. I told her you weren't doing so well, but I guess that's not such a surprise." Peggy was our neighbour who lived across the road from Mum and had done ever since I can remember. She practically lived at our house, perched on a stool at the breakfast bar in the kitchen, dunking biscuits in her mug of tea as she filled us in on all the gossip that was doing the rounds in our street.

"I'm all right. Just can't seem to get motivated."

"No one expects you to be the life and soul of the party. Have you any idea when you're going back to work yet?"

"No, I haven't agreed a date. Val is being really good and has told me to go back when I'm ready."

"Well, maybe going back to work might be a good idea, take your mind off things, concentrate on something else other than Sasha."

"Oh, I don't know Mum. I can't even dress myself, let alone go out to work. Maybe if I just went in my pyjamas."

"Oh, you can't do that, love. You haven't got the best collection of pyjamas to go to work in."

"I was joking, Mum."

Good grief, I was making a joke. I can't believe it. The last thing I felt like was cracking jokes. Every morning when I wake up, for the first few seconds, I forget about Sasha and what's happened and then it hits me like a ton of bricks. It's like somebody's punched me in the stomach. Sasha isn't here any more. I have to keep telling myself that.

Mum's voice brought me out of my reverie. "Has Sasha's mum said when the funeral is yet? You know me and your dad would want to go."

"It's on the twenty-sixth May at the church in Heworth." It was the week before we were due to go on holiday to Menorca. I'd already got the tickets in the post and had briefly glanced at the emails I'd received from the holiday company telling me that 'my holiday is almost here'. Me and Sasha would have been so excited. Instead, every time I thought about it, I felt sick to my stomach. That holiday would have been so good.

"Oh, well. At least you've got a date now. I'll tell everybody in the street because I'm sure lots of people will want to attend. Sasha was well thought of around here."

I couldn't speak as a new wave washed over me. Tears sprung to my eyes as I had an image of Sasha as a little girl, about five years old, who had come to my house for the first time for tea. Sasha looked so scared as her mum had stood on the doorstep and dropped her off. Mum had ushered her in and offered her a chocolate biscuit and a glass of milk. From that moment, Sasha became a regular visitor to our house and we made sure we had some chocolate biscuits in the cupboard so we never ran out when Sasha came to visit. She was such a cute, pretty little thing. I couldn't bear it. I thought my heart would break.

"Erin… Erin, love, are you still there?"

"Yes, Mum, I'm here. I just get a bit tearful every so often, I'm sorry, I had a moment."

"I guess you'll have lots of moments to come. Once the funeral is out of the way, you can start afresh. Although there will be an awful sadness in your heart, you will find each day becomes more bearable until eventually, you will think of Sasha and only good memories and laughter will spring to mind."

"Oh, Mum, I hope you are right."

"I know I'm right. I've lived through many deaths and funerals of close friends and neighbours over the years and it does get easier."

"I just can't seem to get it together at the moment. Nothing seems important. I don't care about anything, especially myself. I can't eat. I just sleep. It's only your phone calls each day that keep me going."

"You've got to pull yourself together, girl. Sasha would be looking down on you and shaking her head. She wouldn't expect you to fall apart like this. She would probably shout at you and tell you to get a grip, Erin. Life goes on."

"You're right, Mum. Sasha wouldn't behave like this. I'll get a shower, get dressed and make myself something to eat and then I will ring Val and tell her I'll go back to work on Monday."

"Good, that's more like it. I think it will do you good."

"I hope so, I really do."

Chapter 12

I went back to work on Monday. It was awful. I kept looking up, expecting to see Sasha sat opposite me, but she wasn't there. I missed her so much and found myself talking out loud to her, as if she was still there. She never answered back, of course, but it helped me.

Trevor had phoned me a couple of times. I think he'd heard what had happened and had called to check I was OK. It was quite nice really. He didn't try to ask me on another date, I think that had run its course.

Val was off work at the moment. She was undergoing another round of IVF and today they were putting the eggs back in her. She had to lay down and relax for a couple of days and hope that the eggs did their best. I really hoped it worked for her this time; it was the last chance they had. They had run out of money now, having spent over twenty thousand pounds on treatments. Everyone at work who knew what Val was going through had their fingers crossed. A new life potentially. Someone dies and another one is born and takes their place. The circle of life, I suppose.

I was on autopilot, making my way through the pile of work. I sent loads of emails, typed lots of reports, enrolled people on various courses and organised seminar rooms for meetings and lectures.

The rest of the week was spent doing pretty much the same sort of thing. I worked with my head down and got on with things. I found if I kept myself busy, it took my mind off things. I got through so much work. I was in a little world of my own, replaying a montage of clips in my head of times I had shared with Sasha. I found myself in tears many times. A couple of people had come into the office for something and had seen me crying and respectfully left me to it. They would come back later.

Mum had invited me for tea that evening. I think it's her way of trying to make tomorrow a little bit easier. Tomorrow it's Sasha's funeral and I'm dreading it. It would be the first time I've seen Ben since our night out, and all of Sasha's family, including her mum and dad and brother, Andy. I don't know what to say to them all. They must be feeling even worse than I am, though I couldn't imagine how they could feel any worse.

I walked to Mum and Dad's house, it wasn't too far. When I got there, I saw Adam's car parked on the road outside. He must have been invited too, and probably Sarah.

"Hi, only me," I shouted as I opened the door.

"Hi Rin, we're in the lounge," came my brother's voice from the front room.

I kicked my shoes off and put them neatly by the door and made my way to the lounge.

Mum, Dad, Adam and Sarah were all sat in various chairs, each with a cup of tea in their hands.

"Do you want a cup of tea?" asked Mum.

"No thanks. I can't seem to keep anything down at the moment."

"Oh, love. You're wasting away. Let me get you something to drink, juice?"

"Juice would be good, thanks."

Mum went off to the kitchen and came back shortly after with a glass of apple juice and passed me it.

"Thanks, Mum."

"Are you all set for the funeral tomorrow?" asked Adam who sat and drank his tea while he waited for me to take a few mouthfuls of my drink.

"I've just got to go back home tonight and finish off the montage of pictures I've put together."

"What's it for? Where's it going to go?" Sarah asked me.

"It's to go at the back of the church for people to look at before the service takes place. I've got so many pictures of Sasha, I still need to sort through them all and pick out the best ones."

"I'm sure you'll do a brilliant job, love," Dad responded.

"I hope so, Sasha deserves it." We all sat in contemplative silence for a few moments while we enjoyed our drinks.

"To change the subject onto more positive things, I still need to find out whether you're going to do some pictures at Tracey's wedding in September," Mum asked. "And how much you'll charge?"

"Yes, of course I'll do some. Tell her I'll do them for fifty pounds, mates' rates."

"Mates rates or not, that's way too cheap. I was thinking you should charge her at least five hundred pounds. That's what she is expecting, so go for it," Mum stressed.

"OK, tell her five hundred. I've got the dates in my diary, so tell her I'll be there."

"Good, that's better, I'll let her know." Mum smiled.

"Tracey's only gone and invited that girl, Keira, from down the road to her evening do. She's a right one is that Keira, always flirting and flaunting herself. She's gaining a right reputation, and not a good one. She's always wearing things that don't leave much to the imagination, if you know I mean. She wore a top the other day that barely held her boobs in. She was parading up and down the street in front of all the boys. Don't get me wrong, they loved it, but they don't stand a chance of copping off with her. I don't know, she's one of those girls. What do you call them? I know, trick pease, that's it!"

Adam sniggered behind his hand. "That's a good one, Mum, I've not heard that one before. 'Trick pease'. That's got to be one of your best, Mum!" At that point, the whole room erupted in laughter. Even I started to laugh!

"What, what have I said?" questioned Mum. "Oh well, whatever I said it was worth it to see you all laughing."

"Adam, there's a plate of sandwiches in the kitchen, can you bring them in, love. I only made sandwiches for tea. I didn't think people would want a full dinner." Adam came back with a big plate of sandwiches and placed them down in the middle of the table. Mum had made a lovely selection of ham, cheese, tuna and chicken sandwiches.

"Oh, Mum they look lovely, but I don't think I can eat anything, I'm just so nervous about tomorrow".

"You need to eat something, love, you'll end up passing out." I noted the frown creased on her eyebrows.

So, I took a couple of chicken sandwiches from the plate and put them in front of me. I didn't want to hurt Mum's feelings. I pulled the crusts off the bread and then nibbled at the sandwiches, the bread getting stuck in a lump in my throat. I used what was left of my apple juice to help swallow the lumps down. I tried my best. At least I'd finished my drink.

"Right, I'd better get going. I've still got a mountain of photographs to sort through and put together for this montage. I want to do Sasha proud," I said as I pulled my chair away from the table.

"But you've barely touched your sandwiches, love," stated Mum. "And I've got a lovely chocolate cake for pudding."

"Yes, Mum, you've done a lovely spread, but I really can't eat anything else," I replied.

"Well at least take some chocolate cake home with you, have it later if you fancy." Mum disappeared in the kitchen again and came back moments later with a piece of chocolate cake wrapped in tin foil. "There, take that with you and try to eat a bit later."

"Thanks, Mum. I'll try to eat it, I promise. Now, let me get back to my photo montage," I told her.

"OK, love. I'm sure you'll do a lovely job. I'm looking forward to seeing it tomorrow," dad said as he munched on his ham sandwich.

"We'll see you tomorrow at the church, just before eleven. I'm sure there's going to be a lot of people there. Sasha was certainly well thought of around here."

"Yeah, sis, we'll see you tomorrow. Chin up," agreed Adam.

"I'll see you there," I replied, feeling myself filling up with the prospect of tomorrow's funeral.

I put on my shoes, closed the front door and walked slowly back to my flat, my mind full of thoughts of Sasha. Always Sasha. The missing piece of my puzzle. The other half of me. I miss you so much Sash.

I put the piece of chocolate cake on the kitchen side. I intended to eat it later, after I'd finished my picture display. It was still there, uneaten, when I went to bed at midnight.

Chapter 13

*I*t was the day of the funeral. I was dressed in the brightest, boldest, most colourful outfit I could find. Sasha would die (bad choice of words) if she knew everybody was wearing black for her funeral. She'd always said it was depressing when people wore black to a funeral. It was supposed to be a celebration of their life, not a group of people dressed in black, acting all sad and depressed. Sasha's mum, Pauline, had indicated to everyone that they should wear something bright and colourful, just like Sasha. Black was banned. I couldn't agree more.

I arrived at the church quite early, just to make sure I had plenty of time before the service began. I brought my photo display with me and went straight into the church to put it up. The vicar was a lady (I've never met a female vicar before) who came rushing across when I got through the door.

"Hello, you must be Erin?" she asked. "I'm Lydia."

"Hello, nice to meet you," I greeted her. "I was wondering where I should set up my photo display?"

"Oh yes, Pauline told me you were bringing a display of photos with you. You can put it here near the door, so people can have a look when they walk in."

I opened my portfolio and took out the pages I had carefully made filled with images of Sasha. I spread the pages all over the large, deep mahogany table near the entrance to the church. There were lots of pages to look at. No surprise really, I had an awful lot of photographs. There were pictures when we started school at the age of four, right up to a couple of weeks ago, when I'd taken a photo when we went out for lunch. I added some drawings I'd sketched of Sasha over the years, ones in which I thought I'd captured her perfectly. I briefly rested my fingers on a photograph of Sasha's face. Just touching an image of her made me feel more connected, like I could send her a message through my fingertips into her body. "We can do this Sash," I whispered.

"Oh, my, that is beautiful," smiled Lydia. "Thank you so much for putting that together." Lydia was gazing down at pictures of Sasha.

"I must admit it was painful going through all the pictures I had of Sasha to make this. In a way, I enjoyed it, too. It was quite a cathartic experience."

"Yes, it must have been hard. But it really sums Sasha up. I only had the pleasure to meet Sasha a handful of times, but I'm really getting an insight into the beautiful woman she was when I look at these photographs and drawings."

I finished laying out the display and made my way to sit down, not at the front of the church, that was reserved for Sasha's family, but three rows back, so I had a good view.

The church started to fill up, but I kept my head down. I couldn't face talking to anyone. I glanced up occasionally and caught sight of lots of people I knew, and also Sasha's mum, dad and brother. They looked awful, truly grief stricken. I couldn't do this. I had a lump in my throat the size of a grapefruit, I could barely speak.

I was quite grateful that nobody approached me. People seemed to be silent before the funeral actually began. The church organ started playing quietly in the background as more and more people sat down. There were so many that it was standing room only at the back of the church. I could see people looking at my display. Lots of people were blowing their noses and wiping their eyes.

The organ music rose up and everybody got to their feet, and so it began. All I had to do was cope for the next thirty minutes. I glanced up from my feet to see the coffin being carried by six strong pallbearers who slowly made their way up the aisle and placed the coffin gently down on its rest. The coffin was decorated with pretty white and pink carnations and spelled out the name, Sasha, on each of its sides. I couldn't believe how small it looked. Sasha was inside that box. My beautiful, pretty, gorgeous friend. She was so close to me, I could almost reach out and touch her. But really, she was gone, the Sasha in that box was just a body, not the wonderful friend that was.

Lydia made her way to the front of the church and cleared her throat. She spoke for a few minutes about how beautiful Sasha was and how God had chosen to take Sasha so young for a reason (hah, that made me laugh. There was no reason why she was taken from this earth at such a young age). How her life hasn't been wasted because, "While she was alive, we had the pleasure of such a wonderful daughter, sister, girlfriend, niece and friend to all who knew her."

A few hymns were sung throughout the service, but I never sang a note. I always find it difficult to sing at a funeral. Who feels like singing, for heaven's sake?

Ben was next up. He wanted to say a few words about Sasha and how much she meant to him.

He made his way up to the front of the church. He looked petrified.

He cleared his throat. He opened his mouth and nothing came out. I could tell he was struggling to talk and my heart went out to him for being so brave.

"Hello everyone. I'm not going to say much. Sasha was my life, my reason to be. I am lost without her." Ben put his head down for a few moments while he composed himself.

"I found some words that I think sum Sasha up..."

Ben started to read a few words from a page that he'd written down. He read out in a strong voice, without faltering:

"If tomorrow starts without me, and I'm not here to see,
If the sun should rise you find your eyes all filled with tears for me,
I wish so much you wouldn't cry the way you did today,
While thinking of the many things we didn't get to say.
I know how much you love me, as much as I love you
And each time that you think of me, I know you'll miss me too.
But when tomorrow starts without me please try to understand,
That an angel came and called my name and took me by the hand."

Those words were the undoing of me. It was such a poignant, beautiful verse that summed up Sasha superbly. There was not a dry eye in the church. I couldn't compose myself any more and the grief came out in great sobs. I was making a complete fool of myself, but I didn't care.

There followed another hymn, I've no idea which hymn it was, I just blew my nose as quietly as I could the whole time. At one point, I blew my nose a bit too hard and loud trumpeting noise came out. It made me smile, even through all the sadness. Sasha would have made one of her dirty laughs to that. That one's for you Sasha. Then followed the Lord's Prayer and then it was over, the church bit anyway. People slowly started to make their way outside to the music that Pauline had asked me to choose. I'd picked 'One Day I'll Fly Away' by Randy Crawford. It was one of Sasha's favourite songs.

The next part was the bit at the crematorium which was for immediate family only. I was glad in a way. I've been to services at crematoriums before and find the part where the coffin slides through the curtains far too painful. I was glad I didn't have to go to that bit. I was already drained from the church service.

The funeral cars and immediate family drove slowly off to the crematorium. The rest of us had been asked to make our way to the hotel near the church where a buffet had been laid on and there was a time for everybody to get together to celebrate Sasha's life and have a drink. It was just over the road, so I walked with Mum, Dad, Adam and Sarah.

"Well, that was a lovely service. That vicar seemed like a nice lady and had lots of lovely things to say about Sasha," Mum remarked.

"Aye, it was a good one. I've been to a few funerals in my time, but that was one of the best. Sasha would have been proud," agreed Dad.

"Lots of people were looking at your display, Erin. It's beautiful. It made me fill up looking at it, thinking back to all those memories we have of her over the years. Enough to fill a lifetime," muttered Mum.

"Yes, it's a fantastic display. It just shows how many years you've had with her and all the memories you have," Sarah said. "You may find those pictures painful to look at now, it's all too raw at the moment, but you will find great solace and joy to look at the photographs and pictures of her in the future."

"Yes, when I made the display, I found it very upsetting and it had me sobbing my heart out, but after a while, the pictures made me smile more than anything," I agreed.

We reached the hotel and made our way to the Ebor suite where we found lots of people had already arrived. There was a large table at one end of the room laid out with a full buffet which included sandwiches, sausage rolls, chicken and quiche, among other delicious looking things. On a different occasion, I would have been launching into a full attack on the food, but today I couldn't eat a thing. My appetite was still missing. Appetite or not, my family went over to the food, picked up a plate and started piling it high. They put that much on their plates, there was no space left. Looking at other people they were doing the same too. It seems funerals made people hungry!

"It's a beautiful spread. Aren't you getting anything, love?" asked Mum.

"No, I'm not hungry. I couldn't face a thing."

"I'm off to the bar, what do you want to drink, love?" asked Dad.

"Just an orange juice please, Dad."

"I'll come with you," Adam told him.

It was nice to see so many people I recognised that I hadn't seen for years. After Dad brought the drinks back, I made my way slowly around the crowd. It was nice catching up with people and sharing memories of Sasha. A lot of those people I hadn't seen since I lived with Mum and Dad. They remembered me from my school days mostly and when Sasha used to come round to play. It didn't seem a sad occasion, now people were laughing, drinking and reminiscing about the good old days. I only felt sad when Sasha's family came back from the crematorium service and I made my way over to Pauline.

"Hello, how did it go?" I asked her.

"Oh, you know, not very pleasant but it was nice. As nice as it could be. Now we just need to remember the happy memories we have of Sasha," Pauline smiled.

"Yes, I agree. Everyone here seems to be having a jolly old time. Just as it should be."

"It'll be nice for you, a chance to catch up with some people you haven't seen for years."

"Yes, I've already caught up with a lot of them. I've just been talking to Mrs Cooper about the time when she caught Sasha and me nicking her bottles to take back to the corner shop. We managed to get eight pence back when we handed them in. We bought eight penny chews with the profits we'd made," I laughed.

"Oh, yes, I remember it well. It was nice of Mrs Cooper not to make a fuss. It turned out that you were doing her a favour because she wanted rid of the bottles herself."

Just then Graham, Sasha's dad, joined us.

"Hiya Rin. It's so good to see you. It was a smashing service. Even though Lydia didn't know Sasha all that well, she spoke some really lovely words." Graham whispered, "I do hope you'll keep on coming round to see us every so often. Just because Sasha isn't with us any more, you're still a part of the family and we'd like to see you, once in a while."

"Of course, I'll still come and see you. You don't get rid of me that easily!" I laughed.

While we were all laughing, Ben appeared. I stopped laughing immediately and reached over to Ben and pulled him towards me in a hug. He wrapped his arms around me and he held me for a long time. I could tell he was crying a little bit and that set me off too. We held each other like that for five minutes or more, both needing the closeness of the other. As we both composed ourselves, I pulled away.

"Sorry," trembled Ben. "I really needed that."

"There's no need to apologise, I needed it too."

"I wanted to say thank you for the photographs, they're wonderful. Your pictures were especially fantastic. I have never seen them before. You capture exactly the essence of Sasha in every picture. Lots of people have praised me on the display. They thought I did it. I told them all that it was you who had the talent, not me," Ben said chuckling to himself. It was nice to see that he was able to laugh at such an occasion.

"It's a pleasure. I've got so many pictures and prints of Sasha, if you ever want to come round and have a look, you're more than welcome."

"I will, that's a promise," agreed Ben. "I've been thinking too, you were both due to go on holiday in a few days."

"I know, it would have been so good. We'd been looking forward to it for months."

"You should still go. I'm sure it will do you some good, have a break and get away from all this."

"Oh God, I can't. It would be too painful, knowing that Sasha should be there with me."

"Please go. Lay on a sunbed, get a suntan, eat some tapas, get drunk. Do all the things you would have done if Sasha was with you."

I didn't know what to say, I couldn't go without Sasha.

"Do it for me. Do it for Sasha. It's what she would have wanted."

Could I?

Chapter 14

So here I am, sat on a plane en route to Menorca, all on my own with an empty seat next to me. Sasha should have been sat there. We would have been so excited, looking forward to our holiday in the sun together. I still can't decide whether this holiday is a wonderful opportunity, or whether the whole idea is crazy.

The plane lurched suddenly and I jumped in my seat. The 'fasten seatbelt' display lit up and a voice sounded over the speaker. "Ladies and gentlemen," the voice said. "We are approaching an area where we may experience some mild turbulence. As a safety precaution, please return to your seat and fasten your seat belt. As soon as we have passed the area of turbulence, we will inform you and you will be able to remove your seat belt. Thank you for your understanding." Sasha would have been absolutely petrified at this point. She wasn't a good flyer.

Apart from a few wobbles in my chair, the turbulence was very minor and the seat belt light soon went out and we were able to unfasten our seat belts. Just to be on the safe side, though, I kept my seat belt on throughout the rest of the flight. The journey was only about three hours long and the rest of the flight was quite uneventful and nothing to write home about. The plane landed smoothly and came to a stop. Everybody started to grab their belongings from the overhead lockers as we prepared to leave the plane.

I first realised how hot it was when the plane door opened as we waited to get off the plane. A wave of hot air hit me and everyone around me started 'oohing' about how hot it was. It was unseasonably hot for the beginning of June, temperatures reaching about ninety degrees.

We climbed down the steps of the plane, and following a short bus ride, arrived in the terminal to collect our suitcases. I hate the whole suitcase pick-up thing. The suitcases crept slowly around the carousel, and despite the conveyor belt going at a snail's pace, people pushed and shoved each other out of the way in an effort to get to their suitcases before they disappeared out of view and the whole journey began again. That's if you were lucky enough to actually get your suitcase. Once, on my return journey, my suitcase had been sent to Bristol airport instead of Manchester. I had to wait three days until my suitcase made its way back home. Fortunately, this time, I spotted my suitcase almost straight away and was able to pick it up it easily.

Following the message board, I wheeled my suitcase to the bus that was patiently waiting in row D-two in the coach park. I handed my suitcase to the driver who almost threw it into the luggage compartment underneath the coach. "Binebeca, *si*?" he asked me.

"Yes, Binebeca. Ocean beach apartments."

"*Si*, twenty-five minute," he told me.

I climbed on board the coach and took a seat near the back and waited for the other passengers to get on. There were a mixture of couples and families with excited children who joined the coach and I spent an interesting ten minutes people watching from my seat at the back. In no time, we were on our way. It was about eight o'clock and the sun was starting to set. It cast a warm glow over the whole island, and a warm glow settled over me. This is a beautiful island. "You would have loved this place, Sash," I muttered under my breath, as I took in the views.

I watched the glorious sunset as we made our way around the twisty roads towards Binebeca. It didn't take long, and after a couple of drop-offs, the coach stopped and the driver said, "Ocean beach". And I stood up. There were a few getting off at this stop. After a few minutes scrabbling around the luggage compartment, the driver reached my suitcase and handed to me.

"I guess this is it?" I said to the lady stood next to me.

"Yep, this is it. Ocean apartments. It's our fourth visit. It's a lovely place, you wait until you get inside. Are you on your own or are you waiting for someone?" she asked me.

"No, it's just me. I was supposed to be here with a friend but she can't make it now," I told her. I didn't elaborate.

"Oh, OK then. My name's Laura. That's my husband, Mike, over there by the drinks machine."

"Hello Laura. I'm Erin."

"Hello, Erin. If you need anything, just look out for us. You'll usually find us in the beach bar drinking cocktails! They do mean pina coladas. You must try one, it'll knock your socks off."

Mike made his way over to Laura. "Mike, this is Erin. She's here on her own. I said we'd look out for her."

"Hi, Erin, nice to meet you," Mike nodded. "Come on, Loz, I've got the keys. We're in apartment twenty-one, the one with the brilliant view over the pool."

"Oooh, lovely. What apartment are you in?" asked Laura.

"I don't know yet. I've still to check in."

"If you're anywhere near apartment twenty-one, keep your eye out for us. We'll probably see you around and about anyway. I'd best be off, catch you later."

Laura and Mike disappeared round the corner as I made my way over to the reception desk. The lady I checked in with had a brilliant English accent and I quickly had my keys and made my way to my apartment, number twenty-two, next to Laura and Mike, I think.

It was dark by now as I put the key in the lock. I pushed the door open and turned on the lights. Wow. This place was superb. The kitchen was decked out with all mod cons, even a conduction oven and there was an ice maker in the door of the fridge. There was everything you would ever need in an apartment. It was far superior to anything I've ever stayed in. "We chose well, Sash. I'd have no problem conjuring up a culinary feast in this kitchen!"

Next, I opened the bedroom door. OMG the bed was massive and there were two of them! It was so sad to think that Sasha should be sharing this apartment with me.

I made my way back to the living room and plonked myself down on the sofa. I wished with all my heart that Sasha was here with me. I felt tears prickling my eyes. "It's not fair, Sasha, you should be here with me," I sniffed. Just at that moment, the lights dimmed, switching off completely for a few seconds before they came back on. Instead of feeling scared, I felt it was a sign from Sasha, like she was there with me, not in body, but in soul. I shook my head to clear my thoughts, I was just being silly. It was just a dip in the power supply.

I then spent the next half an hour unpacking my suitcase, hanging my clothes in the wardrobe and my knickers, bras, make-up and stuff in the drawers. By the end of this, I was completely knackered, and without even getting changed into my pyjamas, I fell into a deep sleep.

The next morning when I woke up, I opened my eyes and for the first time didn't feel the sucker punch to my insides when I realised Sasha was dead. Normally, I couldn't function until lunchtime, I was so swallowed up with grief. This morning, I felt reinvigorated and walked over to the patio doors, pulled them open and stepped onto the balcony. When I looked down, I gasped. It was beautiful. Immediately to my right was the swimming pool, which looked fantastic. It was massive with a whole section dedicated to tubes and slides. There were couples and families dotted here and there laid out on sunbeds taking in the hot sun. Children leapt from the edge of the pool into the middle with shrieks of laughter. When I looked up beyond the well-maintained gardens, I could see the sea stretching for miles in front of me. The balcony had a table and chairs on it. This would be the perfect spot where I could people watch all day long.

I went back into the apartment and picked up the folder on the side table marked *Ocean Apartments — Things You Need to Know*. I grabbed a bottle of water from the fridge (already supplied as part of a welcome pack — that reminded me I'd have to go buy some groceries from a shop nearby) and sat down on a chair outside and started flicking through the pages of the guide. A lot of the info was about how things worked like the dishwasher and the oven.

Further into the binder I discovered that there was a *Welcome Meeting* where you could meet other guests staying at the hotel and book excursions and tours (that was the main reason for the meeting!). That might be good idea, a meet up with guests. Another reason to go to the meeting was that there were refreshments as well (soft drinks, juice, beer and sangria) and a selection of tapas. It stated that there are regular meetings on a Monday afternoon at three p.m.. It was a Monday today so I pencilled it in my diary (in my head) and fully intended going to the meeting that afternoon.

Next, I needed to buy some groceries. It indicated in the binder that there was a *supermercado* just down the street from the apartments. I slipped a pair of flip-flops on and left the apartment block and walked along the street in the direction of the supermarket. Sure enough, after a few minutes I appeared in front of the local supermarket which was, in fact, a Spar. I grabbed a basket by the entrance and started adding the items I needed: water, bread, butter, orange juice, ham, coffee, chocolate (yes, it was essential) and biscuits. I added a few packets of sweets and I was done. It only came to about forty euros, which I thought was quite good.

I made my way back to my apartment and put the things I'd bought into the fridge and cupboards and again, took a seat on the balcony. It was nearly noon and it was already sweltering.

I opened my book. It was a chick lit I'd bought on a whim from WHSmith in the airport. It was a typical holiday romance, an easy read. You can't beat a bit of escapism. The further I got into the book, the more it made me realise how my life was the exact opposite of the girl in the story. There was no romance in my life. One day maybe, I can only hope.

What felt like ten minutes later, but was in fact, an hour, I realised I was a bit peckish. I made a cup of coffee — good old Nescafé instant — and a ham sandwich — damn, I'd forgotten to buy some mayonnaise — and went back to my book.

I was so engrossed in the story, it wasn't until I looked at my watch that I realised it was only a few minutes until the welcome meeting started. I rushed down to reception with seconds to spare. I saw Laura and Mike were joining the meeting, and made my way towards them. There was a spare seat next to Mike, so I sat down and mouthed 'hello' to Laura just as the meeting started.

The rep joined us and introduced herself as Rita. She started to tell us about Menorca, and in particular, things that were local to Binebeca and the surrounding area. She gave various bits of useful information about restaurants and bars and recommended a few places. Then she started to tell us about the excursions on offer (and their extortionate prices). It was quite an interesting meeting and I gleaned a fair bit of information. I filled myself up on the delicious tapas on offer and drunk a couple of glasses of sangria. It seemed like I was starting to get my appetite back.

Laura came over. "Hi, how you doing? Settled in yet?"

"It's a beautiful place, you were right. The apartment is fabulous, much better than the photos in the brochure."

"I couldn't agree more. Do you fancy any of the excursions on offer?" she asked me.

"The only one I fancy (and the only one I can afford) is the sunset cruise. Have you been on that one?"

"Yes, we've done that one, in fact, we've done them all before at some point in the past. We've been coming to Menorca for years. My advice to you, though, is to do yourself a favour and save the ninety euros you'd spend on the 'sunset cruise trip'. Wander down to the beach and find yourself a table at the bar. Grab a cocktail, sit back, relax and admire the view," Laura told me. "It's spectacular and doesn't cost a penny, well apart from the cocktail! Me and Mike are in there most evenings," Laura told me as she looked through a pile of brochures and leaflets that were on the table.

"Yes, you're right they are a bit expensive. I agree with you about the cost. I've got some spending money, but after a couple of excursions it will be gone."

Rita finished talking and people started to form a queue at the desk in front of her, eager to sign up for day trips and cruises. I decided I wouldn't bother with any of the trips. Laura was right, they were too expensive.

"You're right, Laura. I won't bother signing up for any of the trips. I'll just save my money and view the sunset from the beach, as you suggest. I'd best get going. I've got a hot date with a book," I said as I picked up my bag.

"OK, maybe see you around the bar?" Laura queried.

"Yes, I'll come tonight. I'll look out to you," I replied.

I made my way back to my room, poured myself a glass of juice and settled down on the balcony. I picked up my book and within minutes found myself immersed once again in the story. "I could get used to this, Sash," I muttered as I carried on reading.

Chapter 15

*L*ater that evening, I had a shower and got dressed. I put on a beautifully embellished shift dress that was very flattering and suited me (or so Sasha said). I had a meal in the hotel as I was staying on a half-board basis. The meal was really quite nice. I had spaghetti Bolognese and apricot tart for pudding, all washed down with a glass of sangria which wasn't half bad. I realised I had splattered the front of my dress with bits of spaghetti sauce. I should really go back and get changed, or wash the stains at least. Bugger it, I couldn't be bothered. Because of the embellished bits on the front of the dress, you couldn't really tell. Life's too short!

I decided my plan for the evening was to find the bar on the beach that Laura had spoken about. I wandered into the main square, full of restaurants and bars. The atmosphere was buzzing. I meandered slowly through the streets until I found myself at the beach. I could see a bar on the far side and presumed that was the one that Laura has talked about. I walked over and sat down on a spare table. Shortly after an attractive man, who I presumed was a waiter, headed over to my table.

"Hi, what can I get you?"

"Erm, I'm not sure," I said as I tapped my chin while I looked at the menu. "I don't want anything to eat, just to drink. What cocktails have you got?"

"They're on the back of the menu," he replied as he turned the menu over. "I can recommend sex on the beach," he said with a smirk.

"Ha, ha, very funny, I'm not falling for that one! Do you do pina coladas?"

"We certainly do. One pina colada coming right up," he replied.

This was lovely. Sitting at a bar on the beach, gentle music playing in the background. The temperature was perfect. The scorching heat earlier today had cooled down, leaving an evening that was just pleasantly warm. I almost felt happy. But then I remembered, Sasha wasn't there.

My pina colada arrived without me even realising. The waiter had placed it on my table and walked gracefully away when he noticed I was crying. I wiped my eyes and took a sip of the drink. Wow, that was amazing. It was really nice. I took another sip and stared down, miles away, concentrating on the sand underneath my toes. I didn't notice Laura until she patted me on the shoulder. I jumped out of my skin.

"Sorry Erin, I didn't mean to scare you," Laura looked concerned. She looked at my face.

"You've been crying, what's wrong?"

"Oh, it's nothing, just ignore me," I replied.

"Oh, come on, Erin, you can tell me what's wrong. I'm a good listener. Is it man trouble?"

"If only it were that simple," I told her and promptly burst into tears.

Laura sat down on the chair next to me and put her arm around my shoulder.

"Whatever the problem is, I always find it helps by sharing it with someone. Come on Erin, what's happened?"

"My friend, Sasha, was supposed to be here with me on holiday but she… but she died last month in an accident. Her boyfriend said I should still go on the holiday we were meant to go on together."

"Oh God no, I'm so sorry, were you close?"

"She was my best friend. I met her when we started school when we were both four. We knew each other so well. Ben said I should still go on this holiday, that Sasha would have wanted me to, but I don't know. I can't help but think it was a mistake."

"I think Ben might be right. Ben was Sasha's boyfriend, yes?"

"Yes, he's a lovely guy. He didn't deserve to lose Sasha either."

"So, tell me all about her. I'd love to hear," asked Laura.

So that was that. I told her all about Sasha. Times we had at school, holidays, boyfriends, nights out, everything. Laura just listened and Mike made sure we had a steady stream of cocktails. I don't know how many I drank, but I think I'd had one too many.

I got tired and weepy when I was drunk. I stopped talking and I shut my eyes and started to drift off.

"I think we'd better get you off to bed," Laura announced and picked up both of our handbags.

Laura and Mike pulled me up with an arm under each of my shoulders and we walked back to the apartments slowly, step-by-step. I don't remember how I got back, I just remember being extremely tired. Laura found my key in my handbag, by which time I was practically asleep on my feet. They helped me inside and laid me down on my bed. Laura pulled a thin cover over me and said, "Goodnight, babes."

"Na night. I am soooooooooooo tired. Night Laura. Night Mike. Night Sasha," I managed to say before I drifted off to sleep.

Chapter 16

I woke up the next morning feeling a little worse for wear. I couldn't bear to look outside for ages, it was far too bright for my eyes. Every time I opened them, I got a shooting pain through my head. I took a couple of paracetamol (thank goodness I remembered to pack some) and sat inside the apartment, drinking coffee, until I felt a bit more normal.

I dread to think how embarrassing I was in front of Laura and Mike last night. I remember drinking quite a few pina coladas until I became depressed and sleepy. I know I started reminiscing about Sasha and how much I miss her. I don't remember getting back to my apartment, though, but I woke up fully dressed in my bed. How did that happen? I think I'll have to track them down at some point today and apologise.

I decided to make my way down to the craggy rocks further out in the bay. I'd noticed a place nearby which intrigued me. I wanted to go and have a closer look, maybe draw some pictures. I packed my drawing things into my bag, slipped on my sandals and set off. On my way through the village, I stopped off and bought a bottle of juice and a ham and cheese sandwich.

It was actually further away than I thought, but when I got there, the view was worth it. I had read up about this place in my guidebook before I set off. It was a natural cave underneath the cliffs and when the waves hit the bottom, every so often it would throw the water through the upper holes and make mini fountains of water.

I sat for a while and sipped my drink. I watched as a family appeared on the rocks. They'd obviously heard about this place and they stood next to the hole and waited for the water to shoot out. When it did, the kids screamed in delight and went back to the hole, time and time again, waiting for the next fountain of water. I watched for a while, until I felt ready to draw.

I was soon engrossed in my drawing, my hangover a distant memory. I managed to draw a beautiful image of the cave with the water shooting out of the top. I was quite pleased with the picture and laid it down on top of my portfolio. I put a rock on the sheet to stop it blowing away, although there wasn't even a breeze today.

I took a blank piece of paper and started to draw roughly the same image, but at a slightly different angle. Every so often, I took a bite of my sandwich and a sip of water. Time stood still while I continued to draw, so absorbed was I.

I was pleased that I'd had such a productive day. I'd drawn three pictures that I was satisfied with. I gathered the sketches together and put the first two in my portfolio. I held up the latest drawing and compared it to the landscape in front of me. As I held the picture up, I could feel a presence behind me. Someone was looking at my picture. I turned to my left and saw a man staring. I was unsure whether he was staring at me, or my picture.

"You're pretty good. That looks amazing," he said. He was English.

"Oh, thank you," I replied, as I felt myself blushing.

"You've captured it really well. Looks good to me, anyway," the man said with a cheeky grin. He really was quite attractive.

"I'm Alex by the way. What's your name?" he asked.

"Erin is my full name, but you can call me Rin." Why did I let him use my pet name, Rin? The only people that ever use the short version of my name are the people that I love, like Mum, Dad and Adam. Like Sasha.

"Pleased to meet you, Rin." He smiled as he walked up to me with his hand outstretched. I took his hand to shake and an electric shock ran from my hand and up my arm.

"Ow, did you feel that?" I asked him.

"Gosh, that was weird. It felt like when you get an electric shock from a lift button."

"Strange." I frowned whilst I rubbed my arm. At that moment, there was a strong gust of wind which lifted the picture out of my hand and it started to blow away. Alex ran to catch it and managed to put his foot on one edge of the picture. He reached down and picked it up. Fortunately, his Converse trainers hadn't made a mark on the picture. Hmm, nice footwear, I noticed.

"Thank you so much. Where the heck did that gust come from? There hasn't even been a breeze today," I frowned.

"I dunno. At least I managed to catch your picture."

"That's true, thanks for that." I smiled as he handed it back to me.

"So, you're an artist then? You don't sound Spanish, though, so I guess you're an English artist."

I laughed. "No, I'm not an artist. It's just something I do in my spare time. And no, I'm not Spanish. I'm from good old Blighty, York to be precise."

"Ah, so you are English. You do have a bit of a Yorkshire twang, you know 'eee by gum' and all that," Alex grinned.

"Oy, you. Don't be so cheeky. Where are you from, then?"

"Well, I am a Yorkshire pudding too. I'm from Scarborough."

"No way, eee by gum right back at ya! We're both Northerners then. That's good, it feels like we have a connection."

The conversation was flowing. He was so easy to talk to.

"So, if you're not an artist, what do you do for a living?"

"I'm an administrator in a research centre at the University of York. Pretty boring stuff really."

"That sounds a lot less boring than my job. I'm a postman."

"That's not a boring job. I imagine it's quite an eye opener being able to look through all the post your neighbours are getting," I guessed.

"Be nosy, I think you mean."

"No, I didn't mean it like that," I stumbled.

"I know, I was only kidding," Alex laughed. "What you mean is, as their postman, I'm aware of the type of post the neighbours receive. Like, Mrs Butcher from number fifty-six regularly receives the Ann Summers catalogue," Alex laughed. "It clearly means she must be a raving sex addict who likes to dress up for Mr Butcher."

"Well, you never know," I giggled. "But seriously, I feel sorry when I think of my postman in the middle of winter. He has to get up at the crack of dawn, trudge around in the dark and freeze his you-know-whats off."

"Yes, it can be a bit grim in winter but I'm still the proud owner of a full set of you-know-whats," he laughed. "But it's fantastic in summer, with the birds singing and the light mornings. It's great then."

"Yes, I guess it has its plus points. It must be lovely being up and about so early in the morning," I agreed.

"It's beautiful in spring and summer, but I'm taking some time out from work. They're letting me take a sabbatical and I'm using it to spread my wings a bit. I've got a job here in Menorca as a holiday rep. I start on the first of July. I'm just mooching around Menorca at the moment, so I have a bit of an idea as to what the island has to offer," Alex told me.

"So, you've mooched your way over to Binebeca. You like it?"

"From what I've seen so far, Binebeca has a lot to offer. I think so, anyway."

I felt there was a hidden meaning to what Alex was saying. I crossed my fingers behind my back and hoped he meant that *I* had a lot to offer.

I don't know anything about him. Maybe he had a girlfriend already back in Scarborough?

"Are you here on your own, then? Nobody waiting for you in Scarborough," I asked him.

"Yes, I'm here in my own. I've yet to meet the other reps I'll be working with, but I guess I'll meet them on the first of July. That gives me over three weeks to just laze around and get a suntan," he laughed. "No, there is nobody waiting for me for me back home." This just keeps getting better and better. Single and no significant other.

"I've got another six days left of my holiday. I can't believe how quickly time is passing already."

"Is there a Mr Rin back at your hotel?"

127

"No, it's just me. I was supposed to be here with my best friend."

"Supposed to be? Why couldn't she make it? Did she have to work, or something?"

"It's a long story. I won't bore you."

"You won't bore me. I tell you what, you can tell me all about it tomorrow."

"Tomorrow?" Did he mean he was going to see me again tomorrow? Oh, please, please, I hope that's what he means.

"Yes, I'll come back tomorrow, if that's OK."

"I'd like that. Why don't you come to my apartment, it's a bit more comfortable? There's a brilliant balcony we could sit out on," I suggested.

"Brilliant, that sounds like a plan. What's the address?"

"Ocean apartments, apartment twenty-two. It's on the second floor."

"I'll be there, about eleven o'clock?"

"Yes, perfect. I'll see you tomorrow."

"Yes, see you tomorrow. I can't wait," Alex said before he walked back along the track.

OMG. He's fantastic. I can't believe I'll be seeing him again tomorrow. He said he can't wait to see me. Wow, I hope he turns up. Knowing my luck, that's the last I'll see of him. It didn't even cross my mind at how reckless I'd been inviting him to my flat when I hardly knew him. I would let Laura know what I was doing. She'd look out for me.

Don't be so negative I can hear Sasha remonstrating.

You'd love him, Sash. I do wish you could meet him.

That night, I went to the beach bar on the lookout for Laura and Mike. They weren't there when I turned up, so I ordered a pina colada (what else!) and waited for them to appear while I watched the sunset. I hadn't been waiting long when I saw them approaching the bar.

"Hi, Mike. Hi, Laura. I thought you might turn up here," I shouted as I waved them over to my table.

"Hi, babe. It's nice to see you, are you having a good time?" Laura asked.

"Oh yes, I'm having a fantastic time," I grinned. "But first, I wanted to apologise for my behaviour last night. I can't remember it all, but I know I was pretty drunk and talking a load of rubbish, mostly about Sasha, I recall."

"Don't worry about it. You talked about Sasha a lot. She sounded such a good friend and I feel so sorry that she has passed. You didn't do anything wrong. Me and Mike walked you home and put you to bed. It was probably about two o'clock in the morning when we finally left you. We put a bowl by the side of the bed in case you needed to throw up!"

"I wondered how I got into bed. Thank you so much for looking after me," I stressed.

"No worries. We wanted to make sure you got home in one piece," Mike told her.

"Well, thank you both. Let me buy you some drinks. You must have bought all of those pina coladas for me last night." I waved the waiter over and Laura and Mike ordered a couple of drinks and I made sure I paid for them.

"I've got another favour to ask you." I wriggled in my chair.

"What is it, I'm all ears?" Laura said as she pulled her chair closer to mine.

"Well, I've met someone. We're meeting again tomorrow. I asked him to come to my apartment, but thinking about it, I hardly know him. He could be an axe murderer for all I know! I guess I just wanted to ask you to look out for me."

"Oooooooh, exciting! What time is he coming?" asked Laura.

"He's coming at eleven o'clock tomorrow morning."

"Me and Mike will be by the pool at that time, probably until about four o'clock, so we won't be in the apartment."

"We'll probably sit on the balcony, so you should be able see me, I suppose. I just wanted to let you know just in case I disappear and you never see me again!" I joked.

"Yes, at least we know you've got a visitor."

"Shall I ring your apartment tomorrow teatime and let you know everything's OK?" I suggested.

"Good idea. If I don't hear from you, I'll know something's up," Laura agreed. "You'll have to let me know how you get on. It's dead exciting. Where did you meet?"

"We met by the rocks in the bay. I was drawing and he came up and commented on my picture and we started talking. I can't believe how well we got on. He's so easy to talk to."

"What's his name? Is he Spanish?"

"He's English and his name is Alex. He comes from Scarborough, about an hour from where I live. He's about to start a new job as a rep here in Menorca. He's got brown hair and brown eyes and one of his front teeth slightly overlaps the other and he looks really cute. He's so funny, he really makes me laugh."

"Woah, slow down," laughed Laura. "He sounds lovely, but please be careful. Like you said, you don't know him very well. Make sure you ring us at teatime tomorrow," Laura stressed.

"OK, I will. And if I forget, you can always ring my apartment from your phone. You only have to dial twenty-two."

"Sorted. All you have to do now is have a good time," grinned Laura.

"I hope so."

Chapter 17

I woke early the next morning and tried to make myself look sexy, alluring and hot. Who am I trying to kid? I decided to play it safe and just look pretty, attractive and slightly sexy.

I put on a subtle dusting of make-up and blow dried my hair. I didn't want to make it obvious that I'd made too much of an effort (which, I had), so I dressed casually in a pair of shorts and a pretty top.

I ate a piece of toast to settle my stomach and waited patiently. I read my book and watched the time creep slowly around to eleven o'clock. Bang on time, there was a knock at the door. I felt sick.

I opened the door and there was Alex, neatly dressed in shorts and a polo shirt. He'd actually come! Yay!

"Hello, I'm glad you made it," I smiled.

"I was here at ten thirty, but I was scared to knock too early, so I waited round the corner until eleven. I was getting myself in a real state, I can tell you."

"Oh, flippin 'eck, you should've just knocked. I've just been sat here trying to read my book and feeling sick."

"Sounds like we're as bad as each other!" he laughed.

"Come in, come in," I said as I opened the door.

"Wow, this is fantastic. I've never seen such a brilliant holiday apartment. This must have cost you a fortune!" Alex said as he took it all in.

"You should see the bedroom, it's enormous and it's got two beds in it," I told him, and then I blushed when I realised he might interpret it as an invitation to take him to bed.

"Maybe I'll get to look at the bedroom some point in the future," he smiled. I knew what he was implying and blushed even further.

"Do you want a drink? I'm afraid I've only got orange juice or water."

"I'll have a glass of juice, please."

I went to the kitchen and poured us each a glass of orange and poured some crisps in a bowl and managed to carry all three through at once. I was pretty impressed with myself (especially as I was so nervous).

"I guess the view from the balcony is pretty special, too. I think I remember you said it would be a good place for us to sit out."

"Yes, it's really something. Come on, we'll go sit out there now."

Alex followed me out onto the balcony. "This is gorgeous, what a view! You've got a really nice spot here," he said as he took a seat and I put his juice on the table.

"I know, it's lovely. Me and Sasha chose it together last year. We were both so excited. I'm gutted that she isn't here with me now."

"Yes, Sasha. You were going to tell me about her. That's only if you want to tell me that is. You might think I'm being nosy."

"No, you're not being nosy. I warn you though, there will be probably be tears."

"No worries, I'll be on hand with the tissues."

I ran back into the kitchen and grabbed some kitchen roll.

"There, now I have tissues. Gosh, where do I start?"

"Start at the beginning, the day you first met," suggested Alex.

"OK." I took a deep breath. "Sasha was my best friend…" And I began (again!).

Alex sat and listened. He put his arms around me and held me close when I reached a particularly sad bit. I couldn't believe how relaxed I felt with him, despite having only met him yesterday. I felt as if I'd known him for years.

After what seemed like ages, I finally finished. I blew my nose on a piece of the kitchen roll he handed me.

"I must look a real mess. My whole face feels like it's puffed up with all this crying. Not the most attractive look. I'm sorry I went on so much. I think I really needed this, to talk to someone who didn't know Sasha. It feels like a weight's been lifted from my shoulders."

"She almost feels real to me, you described her so well. I can tell she was a huge part of your life. I'm so sorry for your loss. Though, I realise, nothing I can say can bring her back."

"I hope that one day soon I can look back and laugh about the things we got up to."

"I'm sure you will. You've already made a start today," Alex pointed out.

"Yes, that's true."

"There is another thing I can help you with, though," Alex told me.

"And how are you going to do that?" I asked as I looked up, sensing that he wanted to take things a little bit further.

"I can think of a few things," he replied. It was first time I had looked properly into his eyes. They were golden brown, almost black and I found myself mesmerised as I looked deep into them. Alex moved his head slowly towards me and just as he reached my mouth, he pulled back hesitantly, almost unsure. I took control as I leaned in towards him and our lips gently touched. Again, I felt that same electric shock I had felt yesterday. His mouth on mine was just a caress, before he pulled away.

"Sorry, I couldn't help myself," Alex admitted.

"I liked it," I confessed. "Please do it again."

Alex didn't need much encouragement as he reached for my mouth again. He opened his lips very slightly this time and I could feel the tip of his tongue gently touching mine. I reached with my own tongue and tasted him. We kissed tenderly for a few minutes until our kisses became more intense. Gosh, I thought, I could do this all day.

We sat for a while getting to know each other more and exchanging stories before the kissing inevitably started again and each time we stopped before things went too far. We sat on the balcony for hours and I told Alex about the little book of embarrassing moments that Sasha and I had kept over the years.

"Most of the funny things happened to Sasha. I suppose there were a few things that happened to me too, but the things that happened to Sasha always made me laugh more."

"Give me some examples," Alex asked.

"Things like the time when Sasha had gone to the toilet and got a piece of toilet paper, about four foot long, attached to the stiletto heel of her shoe. She then left the bar with the toilet paper still stuck on and we were walking the streets of York for ages before we realised what she'd done!"

"Didn't anyone say anything?"

"No, nobody said anything, but we'd got plenty of sniggers as we walked past. We couldn't work out why, but in hindsight we realised."

"OMG, that's so funny," Alex laughed.

"Then there was the time that Sasha went for her hair cut and it wasn't until the hairdresser held up a mirror to reveal her new hair style that Sasha realised she had a big bogie stuck on her cheek! She was so embarrassed and tried to wipe it away, but it had dried on to her cheek, with all hair drying, so she had to pick it off!" I told him, by which time we were both almost wetting ourselves laughing.

"How come she didn't notice while she was sat in front of the mirror having her hair cut?" Alex asked.

"She's a bit short sighted and couldn't see her face clearly," I explained.

"Oh, I see." Alex understood.

"But I think the funniest moment ever was the time we went for a massage. We were in a dual therapy room, so I was in there with her and enjoying a gorgeous massage. I had my head down, listening to the twinkly pipe music and drifting to sleep when Sasha released the biggest fart you've ever heard! She couldn't help it, she was fast asleep. The therapist just laughed and said it was something that happened all the time. Me and Sash couldn't get out of there fast enough!"

"I bet you couldn't," he agreed. "I've got some funny things that happened to me, but I couldn't beat that one!" Alex said with a massive grin on his face.

"Do tell. What's your most embarrassing moment?" I asked him.

"Well, let's see… The funniest time was when I was watching *Casualty* with my mum and Jim and there was a particularly gory operation which seemed to feature rather a lot of blood. I'm not good with blood, so I left the room and went to the toilet. In the middle of peeing, I fainted and fell onto the floor. My mum found me, trousers round my ankles and nob on display. I was seventeen at the time and was excruciatingly embarrassed that my mum had seen my tackle, things that she hadn't seen since I was about four!"

"Oh, gosh. You must have been so embarrassed."

"Yes, you could say that!"

We talked about our lives and family and put the world to rights. The conversation never seemed to stop or falter. The light faded as the day turned into night, so engrossed we were in each other's tales. We spent the evening locked in each other's arms, kissing and holding hands. It felt magical.

Suddenly, the moment was broken by the shrill ringing of the telephone. I felt confused at first, I couldn't work out what the noise was, and then I realised.

I made my way quickly over to the phone and picked it up. "Hello," I said. But I already knew who it was.

"Laura, is that you?" I asked down the phone.

"Erin, are you OK?" came Laura's concerned voice down the end of the line.

"Yes, it's me. I'm sorry, I totally forgot to ring you."

"As long as you're OK. I did see you on the balcony, so I knew you were still alive! Are you sure everything's all right?"

"Everything is totally OK. Thank you so much for checking up on me. Alex is here now and we're just chatting, and stuff."

"I presume there's been rather lots of 'stuff' as you put it. As long as you're OK, I'll let you get on with it," Laura said. I could tell she was smiling as she spoke.

"I'm fine. Totally fine." I smiled into the phone.

Laura put the phone down. I am so blessed to have found a friend like Laura. I couldn't thank her enough. I made my way back to Alex with a smile on my face.

Alex was still sat on the balcony. "I'd love to stay at bit longer, but I think it's best if I stop now before things go too far."

My heart sank. I was so disappointed. I could still taste his mouth on mine. I felt an irresistible pull towards him. I had never had such strong feelings towards someone so quickly. I just hope he felt the same way about me.

"Oh, OK then. But do I get to see you again?" I asked anxiously.

"Yes, you don't get away that easily," he said with a grin.

"When?"

"We can meet again tomorrow. I'll put something together and we can have a picnic. Why don't we meet by the rocks where we met yesterday?" Alex asked.

"Yes, I'd like that," I replied, my heart soaring. He wanted to see me again. Yes, thank you I said to myself.

"I'll meet you at lunchtime, say one o'clock. I'll bring the food and a bottle of wine and we can have a picnic. Do you like smoked salmon?"

"Yes, I do."

"That's good. I'll make some smoked salmon and cream cheese bagels. And something for pudding."

"Sounds delicious. I can't wait."

"Neither can I," Alex said as he made his way to the door. He leaned in for another kiss. "I'll see you tomorrow, same place, around one." I watched him walk away. I missed him already and he'd only been gone seconds! Get a grip Erin. Thinking about it, it was probably a sensible idea putting a hold on tonight's proceedings. If he'd have stayed much longer, I'm sure we'd have ended up in bed together. I would never normally sleep with somebody so soon, but I wanted him, of that I knew for certain. I really hope he'll be there tomorrow. Fingers crossed.

"You'd like him, Sash. I can't wait to see him again tomorrow," I said out loud. I must stop talking out loud to no one. People will think I'm mad!

I looked at my watch and saw it was only nine o'clock. Too early to go to bed yet, so I had a cool shower and got changed. I was feeling rather hot and sweaty. I don't know whether it was the weather or it was my snogging with Alex that heated me up. I put on a pretty paisley dress with a pair of silver sandals. Putting on a slick of mascara and some lip gloss, I went down to the beach bar to see if I could see Laura and Mike. There was no sign of them, so I sat on my own at a table overlooking the sea and drank a few too many pina coladas again. This time, I made my way back to my apartment on my own, stopping to sit on a wall (well, I say 'sit' on the wall, but it was rather a case of I fell on top of the wall) to watch the sea. It was magnificent, with the moonlight reflecting on the water. "It's beautiful Sash, I wish you could see it." And at that moment, a dolphin jumped out of the water. For a split second, the moonlight shone on the dolphin's skin, making it seem almost ethereal, before it gracefully landed back in the water with an almost silent plop. I took it as a sign from Sasha. I knew I was being foolish, but it helped the ache in my heart to believe.

Inside my apartment, I took my book and sat on the balcony and read for a while. After three pages I couldn't keep my eyes open and made my way to bed. "Night, night Sash," I managed to say as I lay down on the bed, closed my eyes and fell asleep.

Chapter 18

$\mathcal{M}$y plan of action for the morning was to make myself beautiful (preferably drop dead gorgeous). First, I had a shower (making sure I shaved everything that needed shaving, if you know what I mean) and washed my hair. I laid out my favourite (casual) outfit on the bed, making sure it was crease free, and rubbed my skin with scented moisturiser which made my skin smell (and taste!) delicious. I cut and filed my nails (including my toes) and painted them a deep red colour. I took ages on my hair until it looked bouncy and full of life before I gave it a quick squirt of hairspray. I put on my make-up slowly and carefully, choosing colours that were warm and bright, but subtle and not garish. Once I was fully prepped, I put on my dress and stood back and looked at my reflection in the full-length mirror. Not too bad, I thought to myself. I hope Alex turns up. I would hate to have gone to all this trouble for nothing.

I sprayed myself with my favourite perfume, put my drawing paraphernalia under my arm and set off. I must have looked quite comical walking along with a stupid grin on my face. I couldn't help it. I kept remembering moments we'd shared yesterday as we'd cuddled up together.

I reached the rocks where we'd agreed to meet. I looked at my watch, it was only noon and Alex said to meet about one so I had an hour to kill. I took my pastels out and started drawing, but this time focusing more on the beach.

I was totally engrossed and the next time I glanced at my watch it was one fifteen. I looked around to see if I could see Alex, but he was nowhere to be seen. My heart sank. That was it then, he's not coming. I was a fool to even think that he would turn up.

I couldn't be bothered to do any more drawing, my heart wasn't in it, so I packed my stuff away and was just about to set off back to my apartment when I jumped out of my skin when someone shouted, "Boo", behind me. It was Alex.

"Where have you been? It's nearly one thirty. I thought you weren't coming. I was just about to head back." I was trying to be serious but I couldn't keep the smile from my face.

"Sorry, the bus I was on broke down so I had to wait for a new bus. I didn't take your mobile number so I couldn't ring you."

"Never mind, you're here now."

"You're looking gorgeous, by the way."

I blushed, all of a sudden feeling very self-conscious.

"I've brought the picnic. Where shall we eat?" Alex asked.

"Let's walk up this pathway a little bit and we can eat somewhere along there. The sky is looking a bit ominous though, it looks like it could rain." I frowned as I walked along the track.

"Yes, the forecast was a bit poor. It said we could get hit by a storm. Heavy rain and strong winds. I guess we'd better eat quickly."

We walked up the path for a few hundred yards and came across a level bit of ground which was perfect, and very private. Alex pulled out a blanket from the basket and spread it out on the ground. We each sat on a corner while Alex laid out all the food.

"This looks fantastic," I said as I looked at all the food. There were smoked salmon and cream cheese bagels, crisps, olives, salad and cheese. There were strawberries and clotted cream for afters and Alex was in the process of filling two glasses with prosecco.

"There's also some chocolate brownies in the basket if you'd prefer those to strawberries. Or maybe as well as," Alex grinned.

"Wow, what a feast, thank you," I said as I reached for a bagel.

Alex opened a packet of crisps. "Enjoy," he said as he threw a crisp into his mouth.

"This is delicious," I managed to say between mouthfuls.

The sky looked even blacker. A cloud moved over the sun and the temperature dropped. We'd managed to eat maybe half of the picnic before big fat raindrops started to fall from the sky. There was a crack of thunder, followed by a flash of lightning.

"OMG, let's grab the picnic stuff and go back to my apartment. We can stay out of the rain there." We threw the leftover food in the basket, along with the blanket, by which time the rain was torrential. We were soaked through to the skin within seconds. So much for doing my hair and make-up. I bet I looked horrendous.

Alex started laughing louder and louder. His laugh was infectious and it didn't take me long to start laughing along with him. We looked like a pair of drowned rats. I didn't care any more as Alex grabbed me and pulled me close to him. He looked into my eyes and kissed me. I kissed him back.

"Quick, let's get to your apartment," he shouted.

We ran back, the whole time whooping and laughing. There weren't many people out in the rain (sensible, huh?) so there was no one to witness our comical run.

We reached my apartment and I opened the door. We stood in the hallway, dripping all over the floor.

"I'll get some towels, hang on. Maybe if you take off your shirt and shorts and I'll stick them in the tumble dryer. They'll be dry in no time."

"OK, I haven't got any underwear on though, I warn you."

"Oh, I'll get you a dry towel. No I won't, I know, I'll get you one of the bathrobes hanging on the door in the bathroom."

I ran to the bathroom and took two towels off the radiator and slung them over my shoulder and then pulled both of the bathrobes from their hooks on the door and squelched my way back to the hallway.

"Here you go, put one of these on—" I stopped short. There was Alex, totally naked, his shirt and shorts lying in a heap on the floor. I dropped the towels and bathrobes.

"Hadn't you better take your clothes off too? You'll be getting cold."

Alex walked to my side and started to unzip my dress at the back. It had a halter neck top which he pulled over my head and the dress dropped to the floor. I kicked my sandals off and stood naked in front of him. I wasn't wearing any underwear either. The very fact that we were both looking at each other with no clothes on whatsoever made me feel so horny. His gaze ran up and down my body and I could tell he was aroused too as his cock started to twitch and grow.

"You're beautiful," Alex whispered. My nipples were hard and cold as he pulled me to his chest. The feeling of flesh on flesh was so erotic. Alex put his mouth on mine and we started to kiss, tenderly at first and then more urgently. I could feel my body reacting to his, my back arching as his hands moved to cup my bottom and he pulled me closer. I could feel the

146

hardness of him pushing against my belly. I wrapped my arms around him and pulled myself harder against his body.

Alex kissed my neck and worked his way down my chest until he reached my breasts and gently nuzzled each nipple before he took one in his mouth and teased it with his tongue, taking soft, gentle bites. His hands started heading down, slowly, oh so slowly until he finally reached the centre of me. I was wet and ready for him.

His hands finally reached between my legs and he started to rub my clitoris. I let out a moan and this seemed to encourage him further. The sensation was unbearably good as I felt my orgasm building. "No, stop," I said. Alex looked up, confused. "I want to feel you inside me," I gasped and reached down with my hand to meet his hard, solid, cock. Now it was Alex's time to moan as I guided him inside me.

He lifted me up slightly so he could enter properly and started to slide his hard length inside me. I cried out, almost in pain, but the pain was ecstasy, not hurt. We made our way down on the wet floor where we made love. It only took a few moments before we both climaxed at the same time, letting out a cry as we both reached orgasm together.

We lay on the floor, our limbs entwined. After a while, I began to feel cold and uncomfortable. I stood up and pulled Alex up by the hand and I took him to my bedroom where we lay on the bed. He spooned me and

I felt so safe wrapped in his arms. We lay like that for a while without even speaking. We didn't need words to express how we were feeling.

After a while, I turned to face him and we started kissing again. Our passions flared and we made love again, this time more slowly and tenderly. Afterwards we lay on the bed for a while.

It was getting dark outside, so I guessed it was sometime in the evening. I checked my phone and saw it was 7.06 p.m.

"I'm getting quite hungry, I don't know about you?" I said as my stomach growled. "I'll go into the kitchen and grab a few things. I haven't got much in, though."

"Just take the leftovers from the picnic. There's lots of stuff still in there," Alex suggested. "I don't know what sort of state things are in, though, we packed up pretty quickly, so it might be a bit squashed."

I retrieved the hamper and brought it back to the bedroom. I put it on the bed, opened it and had a good look through to assess the damage.

"There's still lots we didn't eat, cheese, olives and what's left of the sandwiches. Plus, there's still strawberries and cream and chocolate brownies," I told Alex.

It appeared that the rain had stopped our picnic very early; there was a lot of food left. I took everything out of the hamper and laid it all out on the bed and we helped ourselves to what was left.

148

"And there's a little bag here as well," I told him with my mouth full as I reached way back into the hamper and pulled out a paper bag. "There, got it!" I told him triumphantly as I held up the bag in my fingers.

"Oh, that. That's just some gum I carry around with me. I brought some from my stash just in case I wanted some. You want a piece?"

"Sure, what make is it? Sasha was addicted to bubble gum. She always carried some around too, you're as bad as her." I smiled at the memory. "Sasha's favourite was the stuff we used to buy when we were younger. She tracked it down to a retro sweet shop and always made sure she had some in her handbag. What was it called? It was little pink stubby rounds of gum and each piece was wrapped individually in waxy paper and twisted on each side…"

"Anglo," Alex said as I pulled a piece from the bag.

I looked at the piece in my hand and the memories came rushing back. The times that me and Sasha had blown bubbles with that gum.

Alex could see I was starting to get upset, so he made light of the situation and said, "I know, let's see who can blow the biggest bubble."

We each unwrapped a piece of gum and started to chew. This challenge was right up my street. For a couple of minutes we chewed and chewed until the gum was at its optimum bubble blowing texture. Yes, I knew my stuff! Sad, eh? Then we started to blow. Alex was equally as good as me at bubble blowing, but we finally agreed that I blew the biggest bubble that day.

In the end, we ditched the bubbly and started to feed strawberries to each other. I ate the strawberries as seductively as possible (well, I'm not sure if I was seductive, more like ridiculous) and ended up with strawberry juice all over my chin. Alex put the strawberries down and licked the juice from my face. He kissed me so tenderly until he stopped and faced me. "You are so sexy," he told me as he pulled me close. One thing led to another and we ended up making love again. This is ridiculous, I thought to myself, we've had sex three times in eight hours. Not that I'm complaining.

We laid on the bed and talked until the early hours of the morning. We talked about our families and about our friends, things that we wanted to do in the future, our hopes and dreams. Alex told me how much he loved his mum. She'd brought Alex up on her own when his dad left her for another woman when Alex was a small boy. Alex had nothing but love and admiration for her. She did a fantastic job bringing him up and held down three separate jobs trying to make ends meet. She'd met another man, Jim, and they got married in 2010 and have been happily married ever since.

Alex loved his mum a lot and he was clearly proud when he showed me the tattoo he'd had done on his wrist when he arrived in Menorca.

"She hasn't seen it yet, I can't wait to show it to her." He smiled as he looked at his new tattoo. It was a small red heart with 'Mum' written inside in black ink.

"That's lovely. It's really cute and subtle. Do you mind if I take a photo?" I asked.

"No worries, go ahead."

I took my phone out of my pocket and took a quick photo.

I told him about my family and all their foibles. I told him about the silly things my mum said and about Adam and Sarah and how the whole family meant so much to me, especially since Sasha died and I've realised how much I need them.

We talked and talked and put the world to rights. We learnt so much about each other. It was a really special time.

"I never want this day to end," I admitted.

"Neither do I," Alex replied. "So let's just stay here."

So that's exactly what we did.

Chapter 19

We stayed in the apartment for another twenty-four hours. We finished off every scrap of food that was left in the hamper and then moved on to the contents of my fridge (which wasn't a lot). We spent the whole time in bed making love and investigating each other's bodies but there came a point when we needed more food to stoke the fire, as it were. The hotel didn't do room service, so it was left to us to go out and stock up on groceries.

We emerged from our little love nest into the 'real world'. We'd been safely cocooned in the apartment together in total bliss, away from the eyes of the rest of the world. I blinked a few times to get used to the bright sunshine.

We walked to the supermarket down the road to get some shopping and then we planned to explore Binebeca some more. Apart from my initial walk around the square at the beginning of my holiday, I hadn't really explored much of the beautiful resort. Inside the *supermercado,* we loaded our basket with fruit, bread and essentials, enough to last us for a day or two. I realised with a start that I only had another two full days left of my holiday. I couldn't even think about leaving Alex. The thought made me feel sick, so I pushed it to the back of my mind. I would worry about that later.

We wandered through Binebeca, hand-in-hand, stopping to admire the view every so often and sharing a bowl of fruit which we'd bought from a street vendor. After a while, we found ourselves in Binebeca Vell, walking among the myriad of whitewashed streets and tiny, Smurf-like houses. I was attracted to the architecture of the village. I decided it would be great to put some images on paper, so I took loads of photographs which I would be able to draw later.

We turned round and walked back to the other end of the resort and found ourselves at the place where we had eaten our picnic.

"If you wait here, I'll quickly run back to the apartment and get my drawing stuff. The views around here are absolutely gorgeous and I'd love to draw a few more images," I said to Alex.

"No worries. I'll just lay down on this rock and wait for you."

"Brill. I'll buy a couple of sandwiches on my way back and we can eat them for lunch".

"Sounds like a plan," Alex replied as he got himself comfy on the rock. "I'll be here waiting for you. Don't take too long. I'm missing you already," he smirked. "See you in a bit."

I almost ran to the apartment to grab my stuff. On my way back, I bought a couple of sandwiches and some water from the deli on the corner of the square and rushed back. Gosh, it was getting rather hot. It was probably not the best time of day to be sat in the sun.

When I got back, Alex was laid on the rock with his hat over his eyes.

"I'm back," I said as I slumped down on the rock next to him. "I've got some sandwiches and a bottle of water. I think it might be a good idea if we eat them somewhere in the shade. It's much too hot in the sun. Maybe somewhere down there, in between the rocks. That looks like it's in the shade."

We made our way down between the rocks and found a perfect spot out of the sunshine.

"I didn't know what sandwich to buy for you, so I played it safe and got a cheese one," I told him as I unpacked the sandwiches.

"Oh, sorry, I should have said, I'm lactose intolerant, I can't eat cheese."

I was mortified. "Flipping heck, I should have checked. I got a chicken sandwich. You can have that instead. That is, unless you're allergic to chicken too," I flustered.

Alex started laughing. "Sorry, it was a joke. Cheese is fine."

"I can't believe I fell for that one."

We ate our sandwiches in silence. We didn't need to chat, it was just nice to sit with each other.

After we'd eaten our sandwiches, I screwed up the wrappers and put them in my bag. Alex looked at me with a slight frown on his face.

"What's up?" I queried.

"You've got a piece of lettuce on your cheek. I think it's a stray bit of salad that escaped from your sandwich," he said as he reached over and removed it from the side of my face.

His thumb brushed my lip and he cupped my cheek in his hand. I kissed his palm, then his wrist then he moved my head so that he could kiss me properly. The kiss started gently and soon heated up and left me panting and breathless with us both wanting more.

"We can't do it here. Somebody might come," I whispered as his hands slipped under my top and pushed my bra aside so that he could play with my erect nipples with his thumb. I gasped as the inevitable electric shock zinged down my body. I couldn't believe that all it took was a single touch and I was a lost cause. I have never felt anything like it before. The sex was unbelievable and I couldn't get enough of it. I felt myself surrendering. I was wet to his touch and I wanted sex, now.

"Here, Mummy this leads down to the beach," I heard a little girl shout just by my ear. I pulled my top down quickly and tried to make myself look normal. Alex had to pull my bag over his lap to cover up his erection. It would have been obvious to anyone what we had been doing. My skin was glowing and I was breathing hard.

"God, that was close," I whispered.

"Too right, that could have been rather embarrassing."

"I think we should go back to the top of the beach. The views are fantastic up there and I can get some good photos."

We made our way back up through the rocks to our special place. It seemed silly to call it a 'special piece of rock', but it was the place that we first met to eat our picnic.

As I laid out my drawing things, Alex laid on his side propped up on one elbow and watched me.

"Do you ever draw people?" he asked me.

"Yes, quite often. Have a look through the pictures in my portfolio. I get asked by couples to draw people at their wedding reception. I take photographs of guests when they're totally unaware that I'm there. I find that way people are totally relaxed and natural. I then take those images and copy them on canvas."

Alex opened my portfolio and started leafing through the drawings inside.

"Wow, these are brilliant. So, is this something you do separate to your job, a bit of work on the side?" he asked.

"It's just every now and again for people that I know."

"But these are fantastic. You have a real talent."

"Don't you start!" I replied.

"What do you mean?"

"You sound just like my parents and my brother. They're always telling me I should start my own business, drawing pictures for a living, not just for a hobby."

"Too right, I agree. You're wasting a real talent."

"But it's not as easy as that. I'd have to have a regular set of customers. I daren't give up my regular job just on a whim and hope I can make it as a professional artist."

"Sometimes you just have to take a leap of faith. You've already got interest from people by the sounds of it. You should go for it, take the plunge. You won't regret it."

"Hmmmm. I'll think about it." Maybe I should go for it. Oh, I just don't know. I thought to myself.

Alex continued to look through the pictures in my portfolio. He gave the occasional, "Ooh", and "Aah, that's good", and often chuckled to himself when he came across some of the pictures I'd drawn of people in compromising positions.

"These are absolutely fantastic, they're brilliant."

Then he pulled out the picture I'd drawn of Sasha, the one where she was eating the cake.

"Who's this?"

"That's Sasha." And with that I burst into tears, great gut-wrenching sobs. Alex reached over and pulled me into his arms. He held me until my sobs subsided and all I gave was the occasional sniff. He handed me some tissues out of nowhere and offered them to me and in response I blew my nose and sounded like a honking donkey!

"Oh my God, I'm so sorry."

"Don't worry. I think you needed to get that out of your system. Feeling better?" He asked.

"Yes, much."

"In that case, I've a question for you".

"What is it?" I asked.

"Would you draw a picture of me?" he wanted to know.

"Yes, I'd love to," I replied. I didn't need much encouragement to draw so I grabbed my paper and pencils and asked him to sit still.

"You want me to pose?"

"No, don't pose, just look out to sea. Look like you've spotted something really interesting, a boat on the water or a bird and you're keeping your eyes on it. That way I should get a natural pose from you and I can go from there," I explained.

Alex sat on 'our rock' and looked out to the sea. I was able to copy his features perfectly. He sat still for a while and I took the opportunity to just look at him. I knew his face so well, yet it was strange because, in reality, I'd known him for such a short time.

After a while, he complained that his back was aching from holding his position for such a long time (well, his 'long time' was about twenty minutes). But twenty minutes was plenty of time for me to draw a rough sketch and I then started to draw him from another angle, this time laid flat on his belly.

"What are you doing?" I queried. I could see him using a stone to scratch something on the surface of the rock.

"I'm just scratching our initials into the rock. They'll stay there for years, a memory of our time here."

"Aww, that's lovely," I replied as he slowly scratched away.

We stayed like that for ages, me drawing and him scratching. Alex kept humming to himself as he scratched. Every time I recognised a tune, I would join in, and we sat there perfectly happy, singing together. We probably sounded like a pair of screeching cats!

After a while, I heard Alex humming a song that I recognised, a song that meant so much to me.

"'One Day I'll Fly Away' by Randy Crawford," I said as tears sprung to my eyes. Oh, good grief, I was crying again.

"Yeah, it's one of my favourite songs, ever," answered Alex and continued to sing it perfectly. He knew all the words.

"It was Sasha's favourite song," I whispered as the tears rolled down my cheeks. Alex continued to sing the song, oblivious to my tears. I tried to join in with the lyrics, but my voice kept cracking. I thought my heart would break. So, this was Alex's favourite song? It was

Sasha's favourite song too? They were so similar, it was unbelievable.

Alex became aware that I was crying and rushed over. He pulled my face to his and started to kiss the tears on my cheeks. The kisses were gentle at first but became more insistent as he moved to my lips. I felt the inevitable pull in my groin. It was later in the day now and all of the tourists had gone. Surely it was safe now?

Alex undid the button of my shorts and I arched my back to help him pull them down. He pushed aside my knickers and released himself from the confines of his shorts with his other hand. His cock sprang up, hard and ready. It took all of my will power not to take him into my mouth there and then, I knew he would taste so good.

I could sense Alex's impatience, his need to enter me. He took me slowly with gentle thrusts until he was right up inside me, every long inch of him. His cock was big, bigger than I'd ever had before. We made slow, gentle love on the rock until I pushed my face into Alex's neck as I tried to stifle my cries as an orgasm coursed through me in ecstatic waves. My cries seemed to excite Alex as his orgasm soon followed mine as I felt him bucking and twitching inside me as he emptied his load.

We laid in each other's arms afterwards and watched the sun set. We didn't speak. There was no need. It was perfect.

I had never felt so happy and content in my life.

Chapter 20

All too quickly it was the last day of my holiday in Menorca. I finally had to face the truth that it would be my last few hours with Alex.

I packed my suitcase and zipped it up. The hotel was holding the luggage until my departure that evening. I couldn't believe I only had a few hours left.

We walked outside into the sunshine. It was a beautiful day. The weather didn't match the feeling I had in my heart. We walked hand-in-hand in silence through Binebeca and found our way to our rock. I sank down onto its surface. Even though it was just a big rock, there were two perfectly shaped delves in it which fitted our bodies perfectly. Alex had finished carving our initials and had formed a heart shape around our initials, A and E.

"At least our initials will still be here when I'm gone," I moaned.

"Hey, don't be so sad. You've got my number and my email address. We can keep in touch that way and I'll finish my job in October and then I'll be able to fly home."

"October. But October is four months away! I can't wait for four months until I see you again."

"Four months isn't too long. It will fly by."

"It won't fly by. It will be the longest four months of my life. A whole summer to get through. You'll be out day and night, having a whale of a time. You'll probably meet somebody else and forget all about me!"

"I don't think so. Nobody would be able to replace you. I'll be wishing the four months away too."

The coach was picking me up for the airport at five p.m. That gave us just over six hours together. I didn't want to waste those six hours. I lay next to Alex with my head on his chest, listening to his heart.

"I feel so strongly about you. I've never met anyone like you before. I don't think I ever will. We seem to fit together perfectly," I whispered to him.

"I feel exactly the same. You're like the other half of me. I love you, Rin," Alex announced as he pulled me into his arms. Tears started to trickle down my cheeks and he kissed them away.

"I love you too," I cried.

"Don't cry. We'll be together again in no time. But Erin…" He paused.

"What?" I queried.

"When you get back home, promise me you will seriously look into starting up your own business. You must. You've got such a talent, you shouldn't waste it," Alex stressed.

"OK, OK, I promise."

We decided to say our goodbyes here on the rock, not at the hotel in front of everybody. I snuggled down and held him close. It's all well and good talking on the phone or sending emails, but it wasn't the same. I wouldn't be able to touch him, to smell him. Those things are both precious and I will miss them so much.

We lay there for hours. It was so frustrating not being able to make love, but there were too many people about. Instead, we had to make do with talking and kissing.

We nibbled on the bread and cheese I brought with me, but the food just got stuck in my throat.

All too soon it was almost five and time to say goodbye. We stood up and brushed ourselves down. My limbs were stiff and aching as I stood up and every part of me was resisting the final farewell. The minutes ticked by until we knew it was time to say goodbye. We couldn't bear to be apart, but I knew it was inevitable.

We pulled apart and faced each other.

"I love you. Don't forget about me when I'm gone. I'll ring every day so make sure you've got your phone handy," I insisted.

"I'll keep it in my pocket. I'll miss you, Rin. You're a very special person," Alex said. "Remember, Rin, you promised. Set up your new business. Make a start, I know it will work."

I couldn't bear it any more as our fingertips touched and I finally pulled away. I couldn't even look at him again, couldn't see him through my tears. I walked away as quickly as I could and didn't look back. If I looked at him again, I'd have no choice but to run back.

I sobbed out loud as I made my way back to the hotel. I got my suitcase from the hotel lobby just as the coach pulled up. I handed my case over and watched as it was thrown into the bottom of the bus. I climbed on and made my way to the seats at the back. The radio on board the bus started playing 'Farewell my summer love' by Michael Jackson. How appropriate. I sat in pure misery listening to the words. I thought my heart would break.

"Hello, you. I wondered where you'd got to. We haven't seen you for days, where have you been?" It was Laura. Mike was sat next to her on the seat in front, looking a rather bright shade of purple.

"Gosh, that looks painful." I nodded towards his head.

"Aye, it is a bit. I fell asleep on the sunbed by the pool. Serves me right for not putting any sun cream on my head."

"Yes, what a berk. If he'd have come scuba diving with me, he wouldn't have fallen asleep in the sun," Laura told me. "What's up with you, then? You don't look very happy."

"I've had to say goodbye to Alex, he was perfect and now I've had to leave him behind."

"I take it you took it further than a quick kiss?" Laura asked.

"Yes, we had sex, the best sex I've had in my life."

"Oh boy, you've got it bad. We saw you on your balcony the other day. We waved but you didn't see us. I don't know where Alex was, there was only you sat on the balcony."

"He must have nipped to the loo just as you looked up at me, or something." I frowned.

"Yeah, that must be it. Are you going to see him again?" Laura asked me.

"He's got to work the whole summer as a rep. He finishes in October, then he'll be coming home and we intend to meet up then. But that's four months away, I don't think I can wait that long."

"Four months isn't too long. As soon as you get back to work and start doing your normal day-to-day stuff, it will be October before you know it."

"That's what he said. I just don't think I can bear it," I moaned.

"Where does he live? I think you've told me once," asked Laura.

"Scarborough, I'm not sure where exactly."

"At least that's not too far away. You live in York, don't you?" Laura quizzed me.

"Yes, it's only about an hour away. It could be worse I suppose, he could live in Scotland!"

"Have you got any photos of him? I'd love to see who's breaking your heart so badly," Laura said as she elbowed me in the arm.

I reached into my bag and brought my phone out and started whizzing through the pictures I had of him. Well, it seemed I didn't have that many of him after all.

"There's this photo of him here but it's not a very good one," I told her as I held my phone up to Laura so she could see what I was pointing at.

Laura squinted at my phone. "I can't see anything properly, it's too dark."

"Hang on while I get some of the pictures I've drawn over the last few days."

I reached down to my portfolio. That was one thing that stayed by my side. I especially didn't want it to go missing on the bus on the way to the airport.

I pulled out a few pieces of paper and flicked quickly through them. "Here, that's a good one, he's looking directly at me and you can see his face properly," I told Laura as I held the picture up.

"Oooo, he's quite a stunner! I can certainly see why you fell for him. If your picture is a true likeness of him, he's bloody gorgeous!" Laura was almost drooling.

"See what I mean. He's beautiful," I agreed with Laura as I put the sketch back in my portfolio. I could barely look at his image. It made me miss him all the more.

Just at that moment, the bus started to move. It was only a few miles to the airport so the journey didn't take long.

I was so lost in my thoughts, that I didn't realise we'd arrived until Laura shook my shoulder.

"We're here babes, c'mon, let's go." She took my arm and pulled me up.

I climbed off the coach, got my suitcase and pulled it to the check-in desk. Every step took me further and further away from Alex. I handed my ticket to a very happy and smiley girl behind the check-in desk. She was very polite and doing a great job but her incessant smiling and jollying me through each process was doing my head in. After a while, she stopped being so jolly. She could see she was wasting her time. Probably thought I was fed up because my holiday had come to an end. Yeah, and the rest, I thought to myself.

I realised I'd lost sight of Laura and Mike. I didn't get a chance to say "goodbye" to them. At least I've got Laura's telephone number on my phone. Never mind. I made my way to the airport lounge where I bought a magazine and then realised all of the articles were in Spanish. I'd just have to look at pictures. I bought a drink of Coke (well, it was something pretending to be Coke) and flicked through my magazine until it was time to go to the departure gate. Just as I started to make my way to the gate, my phone rang. Oh, God. It must be Alex. Quick. Quick. I scrabbled around in my handbag, trying to find my phone and just reached it just before it rang off.

"Hello, hello, Alex?"

"Hello, love, it's Mum. Are you OK?" My heart dropped when I realised it wasn't Alex at all and was instead my mum. Then I felt guilty for feeling bad that it was my mum.

"Hi Mum. I'm fine, just about to board the plane."

"Oh, that's OK. I was just checking if the flight was on time?" Mum said as I tried to push my magazine into my bag without spilling my 'Coke'.

"Yes Mum, I'm just about to get on board now so it's right on time. It due to the leave at 8.25."

"That's good then. Me and your dad will be at the airport arrivals about eleven thirty."

"All right then, Mum. See you then."

"Is everything all right, Rin," Mum queried. "You sound very quiet."

"Everything's fine, Mum. I guess I'm just depressed because my holiday has ended."

"You had a good time then? I didn't hear from you all week."

That made me feel guilty all over again. I should have spoken to Mum, let her know how I was. But I was otherwise engaged, thoughts of Mum were the last thing on my mind.

"I had a brilliant time. I'll fill you in when you pick me up later."

"That's good then. I'll hang up now and see you in arrivals about eleven thirty."

"OK, Mum. See you then."

The flight back was pretty uneventful. I managed to fall asleep for an hour or so and was woken up by the air hostess who was gently tapping my shoulder and told me to fasten my seat belt and prepare for landing.

By the time I got my suitcase and walked through to arrivals, it was 11.40. I saw Mum and Dad as soon as I got round the corner. They were holding a piece of card with my name on. A bit OTT, but it made me smile.

"She's there, she's there, look," I heard Mum say as I walked over to them.

As I reached them, Mum gave me an enormous hug. Anyone watching would have thought I'd been away for years, not a week.

"Oh love, it's good to see you. We've missed you loads."

"I've only been gone for a week, Mum," I said to her as I pulled out of her embrace.

"I know, love but I've missed you."

"Well then, did you have a good time?" asked Dad who was stood patiently by the side of Mum.

"Yes, I had a really good time," I replied with a wistful look on my face.

"Well, you'll have to tell all about it."

"Can't it wait until I come round to yours tomorrow? I'm so tired, I can barely keep my eyes open," I said as I opened my mouth and gave an enormous yawn.

"Aye, lass, it's nearly midnight. Let's get you back in the car and you can fall asleep while I drive us home."

I don't remember much of the journey home, I fell asleep the minute the car started and I laid back in the seat with my head full of images of Alex and the tender touch of his hand in mine as we walked hand-in-hand by the sea. The way his lips felt on mine. The way his hands felt on my skin...

Chapter 21

I woke the next morning wondering where I was. I thought for a minute I was still in Menorca until I opened my eyes and saw the familiar sight of my bedroom. It was so nice to be back in my familiar room, but my heart was aching for Alex. I wondered what he was doing as I picked up my phone and started looking through my messages. There were only two new messages, both from Mum asking me to come round for lunch at one that day. The next message told me not to forget my camera with my holiday snaps. I was disappointed to realise I didn't have any messages from Alex.

I put my phone next me on the floor where I could see it in case Alex sent me a message and reached for my portfolio. I took out all of the sketches I'd made whilst I was in Binebeca. There were loads of Alex in different poses. I flicked through them all slowly, remembering the heat on my skin and the smile on my face as I drew. It all seemed surreal, so close yet so far away. My fingers lingered over the sketches. I could almost feel Alex was there as I touched his face, as if all

I had to do was turn my head and he would be there beside me.

I planned to take the sketches to Mum and Dad's. I'd be able to let them see how beautiful Alex was.

I realised it was getting late, so I quickly got dressed, grabbing the nearest jumper I could find, and picked up my portfolio and my car keys and headed off for Mum's. I couldn't help but notice I still didn't have anything from Alex.

It was another family affair for lunch. Adam and Sarah were there, already seated at the table when I walked in.

"Oh, hello. I didn't realise you'd be here," I noted.

"Yes, well. Any offer of a free lunch is good enough for me," Adam grinned.

"We wanted to welcome you back from your travels. Was it hot? What did you do? We want to know all the gory details," Sarah quipped from her seat at the table.

"Yes, it was hot. Really hot for the time of year. One day we had a violent thunderstorm and I got soaked," I told them. My mind drifted back to the downpour that had happened when me and Alex had tried to eat the picnic but failed miserably and ended up running back to my apartment and then we... I realised that I'd drifted off and had a stupid smile on my face.

"You met someone, didn't you?" Adam asked.

"I might have done," I said and my smile widened.

"Tell us more. Oh, please spill the beans," Sarah pleaded.

I took a deep breath. "OK. His name is Alex. He's just about to start a job as a rep in Menorca. He lives in Scarborough, so he doesn't live too far away. We met when I was drawing by the sea in Binebeca."

"Have you got any photos?"

"Yes, I've got some photos on my phone and I made lots of sketches of him."

I got my phone from my back pocket, noticing I still had no messages and started scrolling through the pictures I'd taken when I was there. There were lots of shots I'd taken in Binebeca Vell, but they were all shots of the architecture and the cute little buildings. Then I came across a photo that I knew I had taken of Alex in the foreground but the picture was really poor and a little bit fuzzy and you couldn't make out Alex at all. I carried on scrolling through the photos and there were more and more buildings, seascapes and beaches but there were no pictures of Alex. I'm sure I took some pictures of him, I must've done.

"I can't find any pictures of him on my phone. I must've concentrated on sketching him instead." I reached for my portfolio and grabbed all my sketches of him and passed them around.

"Oh, very nice. He looks lovely," Sarah said.

"He is. He's perfect."

"You sound like you've really fallen for this boy. It's all well and good falling for someone while you're on holiday, but what happens now? Are you going to meet up again?" queried Mum as she quickly looked through the sketches.

"We intend to meet up when he gets back to the UK. That's four months away," I groaned.

"Well, if it's meant to be, it's meant to be. Four months is hardly any time really. It'll go really quickly," said Mum. "I'll go get the dinner. If I don't get it soon it'll be burnt to a crisp."

I tidied away all my sketches as Mum and Adam brought all the food in from the kitchen and loaded the table with it all. It looked delicious and my stomach rumbled. I realised I hadn't eaten a proper meal for quite a few days. Me and Alex had just picked at what was left in the fridge. We had other things on our minds!

"It's a lovely joint of beef I got from the butcher. It was a special deal, only cost me a fiver. He promised me it would cut like butter. And I've made some gorgeous fuck dat roast potatoes," she informed us.

"Duck fat potatoes I think you mean, Mum," I told her. She didn't even realise what she'd said. The whole table erupted in laughter, all except Mum who looked around the table at us all.

"What?" she asked in bewilderment as we all carried on laughing.

The meal, as usual, was gorgeous. I ate too much but it was bloody lovely. I checked my phone again. No messages. I'd ring Alex myself once I got back to my flat.

We cleared the table and I helped Mum load the dishwasher and then we retired to the living room where we all sat and dunked biscuits in cups of tea. I didn't think it was possible to fit anything else in after that humongous lunch, but it's amazing, you just seem to manage to find a tiny little empty space in your stomach.

"It's Tracey's wedding in September. I told her you would do her pictures for five hundred pounds. She is really looking forward to seeing your pictures after her wedding. She told me that she would be prepared to pay a lot more for doing the pictures. I told her not to worry, because you're a friend of the family, Erin only said fifty pounds at first. I explained to her that you should certainly pay more than fifty pounds for your services. I told her that you were hoping to start a business sometime in the future," Mum told me as she was busy fishing out the bottom half of the biscuit that had fallen in after she had dunked it in her tea.

"Don't worry, Mum, it's in my diary, I won't forget. Funnily enough, Alex kept going on about how talented I was and how I should start a business drawing pictures for people."

"Aye, he obviously could spot a talent. He should know, you spent that many hours doing sketches of him."

"I know, but he was interesting subject," I smirked.

"Good grief, anyone would think you'd fallen in love, sis," Adam grinned.

"Maybe I have," I replied with a glazed look on my face. I just couldn't stop thinking about him and found myself drifting off with a sickly grin on my face. I snapped back to reality as I glanced down to my phone to see if I had a message yet. No, nothing. I would have thought I'd heard from him by now.

My tea drunk, my biscuits dunked, I said thank you to Mum and made some excuse to get back to do with my washing. Really, I just wanted to ring Alex.

"Right, I'll see you sometime next week. I'll pop over after work one day," I told Mum as I climbed into my car. Still no message.

I couldn't wait to get back to my flat and ring Alex. I don't know why I hadn't heard from him, but there had to be a reason.

I opened the door and flung down my car keys and put my portfolio back under the sofa. I got my phone out of my bag and sat cross legged on the floor and brought up Alex's number. It was a UK number because the phone was registered in the UK.

I waited for the phone to connect. The phone rang, then went dead and a voice said, "The number you have dialled is incorrect." No, I must've dialled wrong. I punched the number into the phone, making sure I pressed the right digits and pressed dial again and got the same message. "The number you have dialled is incorrect." That can't be. I must've written his number down wrong.

I was starting to feel a little bit uneasy. What was going on?

Instead, I sent him a message:

HI, ONLY ME. I'M BACK AT HOME. JUST CHECKING YOU'RE OK BECAUSE I HAVEN'T HEARD FROM YOU YET. I MISS YOU. I LOVE YOU

While I waited for him to answer, I reached for my portfolio again and started to look through the sketches of him I'd made. On my gosh, he is gorgeous. I reached for my phone and still I hadn't had a message back. Instead, my message to Alex had been bounced back and was marked 'undeliverable'. I tried again and a few minutes later my phone pinged and told me that my message was, again, undeliverable.

What was going on? I scrabbled around in my bag and found the piece of paper on which I'd written Alex's number. I know, at the time, I had taken extra care to write it down clearly and I double checked with Alex that I'd written it down right.

I tried to busy myself with the jobs I still had to do. There was a big pile of washing from my holiday that I'd thrown in a heap onto the floor. I searched through the pile and picked up various items that I know I'd worn when I was with Alex. I pulled each item to my nose and took a deep breath and sniffed. I couldn't smell Alex on any of my clothes, despite thinking his smell would linger on them. So, I picked everything up off the floor and pushed them into the washing machine. I threw in a washing tablet, shut the door and started the programme. I washed a pile of pots by the sink that had grown since my holiday. I emptied my suitcase and put all the, still clean, clothes away. I put a ready meal from the freezer into the oven to cook for my tea. It was macaroni cheese, something which I usually really enjoyed, but it just made me feel sick now. Still nothing from Alex.

The macaroni cheese was ready. I got it out of the oven and poured it onto a plate, got a fork out of the drawer and took the plate over to the sofa and sat down. I sat staring into space as the meal got colder and colder. I only managed a few mouthfuls and put the rest in the bin.

I got all the sketches of Alex and laid them out on the floor. I took my phone again and scrolled through every single photo I had on my phone, looking for one of Alex. On every photograph there was no sign of Alex. I was sure I'd taken at least half a dozen shots of him, but there was nothing on my phone. No photographs to look at, to remember him. All I had were my sketches and the memories as I started to cry.

"Where are you, Alex? Why can't I reach you? Where have you gone?" I cried over and over again until my tears dried up and I made my way wearily to my bed. I pulled the duvet up over my head and closed my eyes, willing myself to sleep. I still had all of my clothes on. Slowly the deep, shuddering breaths eased as sleep overcame me and I fell gratefully to sleep.

Chapter 22

The next day was my first day back at work. I groaned when I woke up and realised I had to go in.

I spent the morning catching up with people and the gossip that I'd missed while I was away. I told them I'd met someone but didn't go into any detail. I couldn't bear to answer any questions about Alex. I think Val could tell there was something the matter and I didn't want to talk about it.

Being back in the office brought home again how much I missed Sasha. Val had moved the desks around while I'd been gone and where Sasha's desk had once been, there was now a bookcase. Although the desk had gone, I could still feel Sasha's presence all around me. On more than one occasion I went to pick something up off my desk and felt a pulse run through my body. It was hard to explain what it felt like. It wasn't an unpleasant sensation, but one which left me feeling somehow cleansed. I couldn't explain it but it happened a few times during that first week back.

I went to Mum and Dad's one evening after work. They weren't expecting me, so Adam and Sarah weren't there. It gave me a chance to talk to Mum about Alex. I'd still not heard anything from him since I left Menorca. That was three whole days ago now.

I knocked on the door and walked in.

"Hello, it's only me," I shouted.

Mum came rushing out of the kitchen, a tea towel in her hands. "Hello, love, this is a surprise."

"Hi, Mum. I've had a lousy day at work, I thought I'd come and see you, see if you can make me feel a bit better," I told her.

"Why, what's wrong?"

"Well, it's mainly because I still haven't heard from Alex."

"Oh, Alex. I knew it was too good to be true."

"I just don't understand it. When we were together, it was perfect. The way we were together was great, he understood me, he seemed to care about me."

"These things usually just fizzle out. It might have seemed that it was wonderful at the time, but maybe he made it seem like that, he knew all of the right buttons to press so you fell for him, hook, line and sinker," Mum pointed out.

"No, I don't believe that. He was genuine," I moaned.

"Genuine my arse," Mum replied. "He was one of those people, just like all the rest. Love 'em and leave 'em," she said, but I didn't want to believe it.

"But we love each other. It was real," I cried.

"Has the phoned you yet, sent you any messages?" asked Mum.

"No, not yet. Maybe his phone is broken, he's lost his phone, or he's lost my number?"

"Stop making excuses. Just face it, he's moved on to his next conquest."

"I came here thinking you'd help. You're just making it worse. Alex is genuine, and I love him. I'll find out what's happened, don't you worry," I cried.

And with that, I left the house, slamming the door behind me. I was distraught. I can't remember the last time Mum and me had fallen out. I got into my car and took a few deep breaths to calm myself.

"I know Mum doesn't believe me but I'll show her, Sash. I wish you were here now so we could talk about it. Mum doesn't really understand, but I know you would."

I started the car and turned the radio on. The station was set to Gallop FM, mine and Sasha's favourite station. At that time in the day, you could dedicate a song. The DJ, Dave Lush, was talking.

"…to a very special friend. This is for you, Erin. She wants you to know she's thinking about you and knows you need a little bit of TLC at the moment, so here we go, this is from Sasha…"

Moments later, 'One Day I'll Fly Away' filled my car with music. WTF was going on? I haven't heard this song for years but now I've heard it once at Sasha's funeral, then again when Alex started singing it, and now. It must be sign, surely? I really believed it was a message from Sasha.

I sat in my car and rested my head on the back rest, closed my eyes while I listened to the song. It made me think of Sasha. It made me think of Alex. Tears rolled down my face as the song played. I miss you so much. I'm not sure who I was saying it to, but it felt like Sasha and Alex were melded into one.

I didn't know what to do any more. What had happened to Alex? He seemed so real to me. I could feel the heat from his body as he held me and his hand cupped my face. I can't believe that I meant nothing to him, that he was just using me.

Once I got home, I took my phone out and rang Gallop FM. The number rang a few times, then it was picked up.

"Hello, Gallop FM, how may I help you today?" a young girl asked.

"Hello. My name is Erin and somebody just requested a song to be played for me. The message was from Sasha. Could you tell me the full name of the person who left the message?" I asked.

"I'm sorry we can't give out that information, it's confidential," the girl replied.

"Oh, but I need to know who left the message. It's really important. I just need to know, please." I begged her.

"I'm sorry, as I explained the service is confidential. I really can't help, sorry."

My next port of call was Laura. I needed to know if she'd seen Alex when we sat on the balcony. I found her number from my address book on my phone and dialled.

Laura answered the phone on the second ring. Hearing her voice took me back to Menorca. It was almost as if I was still there.

"Hi, Laura, it's me, Erin. How you doing?"

"Hi, Erin, it's nice to hear from you. How are you getting on with work now, it's depressing isn't it? I wish I was back in Menorca," she told me.

"Oh yes, I know what you mean. On a different subject, you know Alex?"

"Of course I do, as if I could forget those sketches you made of him, Why, what's up?"

"Did you actually see him sat on my balcony?"

"Well, it's funny you should ask that. No, we never actually saw him. We looked up and saw you lots of times, but never Alex. You always seemed to be sat alone. I commented to Mike that we'd never actually seen him. It was almost as if he never existed."

As Laura spoke those words, a shiver ran down my spine.

"OK, fine. I hope Mike's OK. Say hello to him, won't you. I must go, someone's knocking on the door," I replied as I sank to the floor. There was nobody at my door, I just needed to put the phone down.

I slunk into work the next day. My body was loose and floppy. I felt like I had a head cold. My nose was blocked and I had a gruesome headache. I tried to continue typing a report which I had started yesterday, but I only got down half of the page I was typing on when Val came in, took one look at me and told me to go home.

"In fact, don't come back into the office until you have travelled back to Menorca and sorted out what's happening with this Alex once and for all. You're no good in this state of mind and you need to sort this ASAP," Val insisted.

"But, but I've only just come back. I can't afford to go back to Menorca. It took me months to save for the holiday," I stammered.

"I'll lend you the money, you pay me back when you can afford it. You need to get this sorted once and for all."

"Really? You'd do that? That would be brilliant, thank you." I smiled as my heart started beating a little bit faster at the prospect of meeting up with Alex again so soon.

"Yes, go now, before I change my mind."

It didn't take me long to gather my stuff and leave the office. The offer of the money for a flight out from Val was fantastic. My first port of call was to go on the Internet and sort out a flight. The sooner the better.

I'd only been at home for half an hour before I'd sorted out a flight, leaving tomorrow at one p.m. That would get me in to Menorca by teatime. I would find him, I was sure of it. All I had to do was hang out at the places we'd spent our time. Obviously, not in the apartment that I'd stayed in (that was way too expensive), but I'd managed to book a cheap hotel in Binebeca. I'd just have to hope that Alex was still there. The thought occurred to me that he may have moved on from Binebeca to another resort. I realised with a start that I didn't even know Alex's address in Menorca. We were so loved up, I didn't even ask. What a fool I'd been.

Chapter 23

$\mathcal{H}$ere I was, twenty-four hours later. It seemed strange to be back so soon in such a familiar place. I travelled to the hotel in a coach which was filled with excited holidaymakers, ready for their one or two weeks in the sun. I didn't share in their excitement and just sat at the back of the coach on my own with my eyes shut.

The hotel I was staying in was a basic hotel, one which I wouldn't have chosen to stay for my summer holiday. I didn't need it to be a luxurious hotel, I just needed a base which I could work from to find Alex. This place was clean and ideally situated in the centre of town. This place was perfect.

The flight had been delayed by a couple of hours, so by the time I got to the hotel it was eight o'clock and I thought it would probably be more efficient if I started to look for Alex tomorrow. I hadn't booked a flight back yet. I thought I'd play it by ear and see if I could find him first. I must admit, as each day passed with no contact from Alex, my optimism was turning into pessimism.

I woke the next morning fairly early and ate a bit of breakfast in the hotel restaurant — a fruit yoghurt and a croissant. That was enough for me. I took a couple of the sketches I'd made of Alex, ones that I thought were the most realistic images of him. Sadly, I couldn't find any photographs of him on my phone, so the sketches would have to do. I intended to show them to as many people as I could and ask if they recognised him?

I grabbed the things I needed and set out into the village. It was only nine a.m. and there weren't many people about. Instead, I walked to the shops and restaurants in the centre of the village and started to ask them.

"Hello, my name is Erin. I am looking for this man," I said and I held up the sketches to them. "His name is Alex. He's a rep here, have you seen him?" I asked over and over again.

Everybody shook their head and said the same thing. "No, I haven't seen him."

"He was here with me last week, we spent our time here, did you see us?"

Nobody had seen us. It's like he had vanished. I was getting so disheartened asking the same question all the time and getting nothing back.

Gosh, it was so hot. I needed to drink and went over to the small kiosk in the square. I picked up a bottle of orange juice from the fridge and took it over to the counter to pay. I was putting my change back in my purse and thought I might as well ask the girl who had served me the usual question.

"Have you seen this guy, his name is Alex. He was here last week with me?"

"*Si, si*, I knew him. It sad, I cry," she replied.

"You know him, has he been in lately?"

The girl just looked puzzled. Her English wasn't very good. She started looking around. I didn't know what was wrong with her but she seemed to be frantically looking out for someone else who could help her. About thirty seconds passed and then a woman came through the door from the back into the shop. The girl called her over. They both started talking in rather rapid Spanish. I couldn't make out a word of what they were saying. They spoke far too fast. I do know I heard the name Alex quite a few times. I waited for them to stop speaking.

"Hi, Sophia says you've been asking about Alex?" This lady's English was excellent. I had no problems understanding her.

"Yes, I was with him last week. I am trying to track him down. I need to see him," I explained.

"I don't understand. The pictures you showed Sophia were of a boy who died in a motorbike accident last year. It was a big tragedy here in Menorca. He was from UK. His body was sent back to England to be buried. It was very sad."

"No, that must be somebody else. He must look like Alex. I was here with him in Binebeca last week."

188

I reached into my bag and found the pictures of Alex. "This is who am looking for. I don't have photographs of him, but these sketches are very realistic," I explained as I held out the pictures to her.

"Oh, that's him, Alex. I recognise him. But I don't understand…"

I just looked at her, stunned. "But I was with him, last week. We spent the week together. I love him. He loves me. We were going to meet up in October, when he finished his job. We were going to spend the rest of our lives together. I have never felt so loved…" Oh boy, it was hot, so hot. "I don't feel so good," I said as my knees started to buckle and give way and I slumped to the floor.

I must have fainted because when I woke up, I was in a room I didn't recognise. This must be the staff room in the shop. The girl, Sophia, was wafting a hat in front of my face in an effort to try to get a bit of a breeze on me.

"Are you OK? You fainted. I think you have a bit of a shock," the lady who ran the shop told me.

"I'm sorry, what's your name, I didn't ask?" I asked her.

"I'm Odette. You had us a bit worried there."

It was all coming back to me. They said that Alex had died last year. In a motorbike accident. It was last September. How can that be.

"I don't understand what's going on, there must be a mix up or something."

"While you were out of it, I got some old newspaper clippings I'd kept of the accident. We knew Alex quite well. He often came into the shop for a drink or a sandwich. We were devastated when we heard he died. I kept all the newspaper clippings. I've got them here," Odette said.

She handed me three press cuttings that she'd cut out of a newspaper. I didn't want to look; I couldn't bear the truth. I looked at them. The first two cuttings were in Spanish and I couldn't understand them properly. The final one was in English and I read in horror:

English man aged 23 killed in motorbike accident

It was confirmed today that Alex (Sasha) Alexiou was confirmed dead at the scene of a fatal motorcycle accident. The accident happened on the evening of 21st September and took place on the outskirts of Binebeca when it was understood that Alexiou hit a van coming the other way when he overtook another vehicle. Sasha, as he was called in his native Greece, who was from Scarborough, UK will be sadly missed by all his family and friends. His mother, Sue, was unavailable to comment on the tragedy.

And there it was, confirmation of what the article was telling me, a small picture of the man whose real name was Sasha, but who I had come to know as Alex. I read the article again and tried to comprehend what it was saying. On one hand, it must be true, Alex was dead but on the other hand, I couldn't believe it because I was with him a week ago. I know I didn't imagine it, but...

"What's the name 'Sasha' got to do with it?" I asked Odette.

"Sasha was Alex's real name. He thought it was easier to use Alex as his name to avoid confusion because Sasha was a girl's name to a lot of people, but in Greece, where he's from, Sasha means Alex," Odette explained.

My head was reeling. Could I really have imagined the whole Alex thing? But it had been so real, how could I imagine that? But the Sasha thing was really freaking me out? I'd had a relationship with someone whose name was really Sasha. I'd had weird tingling sensations at work and the feeling that Sasha was there, watching me. Alex's favourite song was the same as Sasha's. A message on the radio from Sasha to Erin. WTF was I supposed to make of this?

I know what I had to do, where I had to go.

"Thank you for looking after me, but I have to go now. There's somewhere I need to go."

"Are you sure you're OK?" asked Odette with a concerned look on her face.

"I'll be fine, thank you," I replied as I picked myself up and got things together, including the pictures of Alex.

I walked to the door and turned back. Odette and Sophia stood there and raised a hand to wave me off as they watched me walk away.

Chapter 24

*T*here was one place I needed to go, to the rock overlooking the sea. We had made love there and laid afterwards in each other's arms in silence, listening to the sea.

It didn't take me long to make my way over to the rocks and I walked down the track towards 'our rock' as we had called it. I could see it in front of me now.

As I approached the rock, my eyes focused on the corner on which Alex had so determinedly scraped out our names. Was it there, or was it just a figment of my imagination? I needed to see, I needed to know.

I let out a small gasp as my eyes rested upon the heart shape around our initials, E and A. I thought it wasn't going to be there, but it was, I hadn't imagined it.

I truly believed that, somehow, I had been in contact with my friend, Sasha, but in the form of Alex. The way I felt with Alex was like I had found a kindred spirit, a friend who knew me inside out, a friend like Sasha.

I thought back to the very last moment I spent with Alex when we said goodbye to each other. The last thing he said to me was, "Promise me you'll start your own business, promise me." Then I walked away. Sasha used to always tell me I needed to start my own business. She had stressed it time and time again, but I'd ignored her. Maybe this was her way of getting through to me?

All I know is that the time I spent with Alex was the best time I've ever had in my life, and I will treasure it forever, even though I realise now it was never real.

Or was it?

Chapter 25

*T*here was one person I needed to visit before I put all of this to rest. I stood on the doorstep and checked the address I'd written on the piece of paper, twenty-eight Elliot Terrace. Yes, I had the right place.

I took a deep breath and knocked on the door. I could hear footsteps coming closer as I stood there nervously wringing my hands together on a handkerchief, something that I'm sure will come in handy over the next few minutes.

Sure enough, the door opened and a middle-aged man faced me. He looked quite friendly and approachable, I hoped I hadn't guessed wrong. "Yes, can I help you?" the man asked.

I took a deep breath. "Hello, my name is Erin. Are you Jim?" I asked him.

"Yes, I'm Jim. Do I know you, it's just that I don't recognise you."

"No, you don't know me, although I have heard a lot about you. From Alex."

"Oh, you must be an old friend of Alex. I'm sorry, didn't you know the devastating news we had last year?

Alex died. When he was working in Menorca in September last year," Jim told me. I could hear the slight tremor in his voice and his eyes were glistening.

"It's OK, I knew about his accident. I just wondered if I could come in a moment and meet with you and Alex's mum, Sue isn't it?" I queried.

"Oh, yes. I suppose that's OK," he said as he pulled the door open and ushered me in.

The way that Alex had described his mum and Jim's house was exactly as I had pictured it. I could see pictures of landscapes on the walls and the little knick-knacks here and there. I followed Jim through as he pushed open the living room door.

"Who is it, love? Somebody selling something?"

"No, nothing like that. I've brought someone in. She said she's an old friend of Alex. This is Erin," Jim said as I walked into the room behind him. This is where I felt the real Alex was. I could feel him all around me as I looked and saw the photos of him scattered all around the room. There was one in which he was proudly holding up a fish he'd caught when he was a little boy. There was a photo of him holding up a medal for some achievement or other and then there was the usual collection of school photos. I even saw the little vase that he'd made his mum when he was about eleven years old. I couldn't help but smile.

"Hi, really pleased to meet you," I said as Jim ushered me into the room. Alex's mum was very small and very beautiful. She had lovely brown eyes and I could see where Alex got his beautiful eyes from.

"Hello, Erin. Nice to meet you. It's nice to meet old friends of Alex's. Where did you know him from?"

I cleared my throat. "Well, I never actually met him, I don't think."

"What do you mean, you've never actually met him? Why are you here then, I don't understand."

"Well, I'm not entirely sure if I understand either. I don't want to come across as a bit of a weirdo, but I met Alex this year."

"You can't have done. Didn't Jim tell you, Alex died last year in a motorcycle accident."

I could tell from Sue's demeanour that she was starting to struggle with my reason to be there.

I started to take the pictures out of my bag that I'd brought with me that I'd drawn of Alex in Binebeca what seemed like ages ago, but it was, in fact, only two months ago.

"I know this is crazy, but I met Alex when I was in Menorca in June, this year," I started to explain.

"But you can't..." Sue started to say.

"These are drawings I made of Alex while I was on holiday, in June."

I handed my pictures over to Sue and she started to slowly look through each one, one by one and handed them to Jim to look through too. When Sue looked up at me her eyes were filled with tears.

"You drew these?" she asked me.

"Yes, I drew them all. Do they look like him?" His mother would surely know?

"Yes," she whispered. "It's like looking at a photograph."

"God, they're a dead ringer for Alex. How can this be?" Jim frowned as he looked at the drawings.

"I don't know, something strange happened. My best friend, my dearest friend, she died in a car accident in May, earlier this year."

"Oh, love, that's terrible. You must have been devastated," Sue asked.

"Yes, it's been an awful time. I still can't believe it and I miss her every day."

"Just like we miss Alex."

"Her fiancé said I should still go on the holiday to Menorca that we'd both booked. I wasn't sure it was a good idea but I was encouraged to go. That's where I met Alex. We fell in love and I spent the best five days of my life with him."

"But how do we know this was Alex and not some random bloke you met?" asked Jim.

"That's a fair point. Alex told me things that were personal to him, that other people wouldn't know," I said.

"Things like what?" Sue asked.

"We talked for hours about his childhood. He told me his dad had left you when he was a little boy and how you'd struggled as a single mum and held down three jobs as you'd brought him up. He told me about

197

the incident when he'd gone to the toilet and passed out and you found him with his trousers round his ankles. And then he told me all about Jim, about Jim being the dad he always wanted. He loved you both so much, that was clear to me."

Sue was openly crying now, a tissue balled in her fist to catch the tears. I didn't want to upset her.

I carried on. "Alex was proud of his mum. Did he tell you about the tattoo that he'd had done on his wrist?"

"Yes, he told me he'd had something done, but he didn't want to tell me what until he came back in October and he could show me himself and get my reaction. But I never got a chance to see it before his cremation because the funeral people told me not to open the casket and look at him because his body was too damaged from the accident."

Sue started sobbing. I felt such respect for this woman. I waited until she'd finished crying and she blew her nose into a fresh hanky that Jim had given her.

"I'm sorry. I just wish I'd had the chance to see him one last time."

"When Alex was talking about his tattoo, I took a photograph of it on my phone. It was so pretty. Would you like to see it?"

"Oh, please. Yes please."

I held my phone up to show her the photo I'd taken of Alex's wrist on which you can clearly see the tattoo, a red heart with the word 'Mum' written across the centre.

"Is that really Alex, though?" Sue asked.

"All I know is the photograph of that wrist is the wrist belonging to the same man I met in Binebeca who was called Alex."

Sue just sat there. I could see her mind was working overtime.

"I feel as if you knew my Alex. You know too much about his life for you not to have met him."

"I did know him. Or I felt like I did. Why would I lie? I have no reason to make this up. I never heard from him again. I tried to contact him but every way I went was met with a blank. I was heartbroken. I'd never met a man like him. He told me you were going to decorate his bedroom for him before he got home. He'd picked the colours, grey and cream and a deep blue feature wall. He told me about the vase he'd made for you at school when he was eleven. I saw the vase, just as he described it. How can I have not met this man? It just doesn't make sense. The one thing I don't understand is the link I had between Alex and my best friend who died. Her name was Sasha. When I met Alex and we touched for the first time, we got an electric shock. There were strange, random gusts of wind which came from nowhere. Alex and Sasha both kept a supply of Anglo bubbly which they both loved and then there was the playing of 'One Day I'll Fly Away' which turned out to be Sasha and Alex's favourite song. Then there was time I was in the car and there was a message to Erin from Sasha and the song they played, yes you guessed it, 'One Day I'll Fly Away' was the song. I just don't get it, I don't understand, do you? There were too many coincidences. They were so alike, they both seemed like the same person…"

I was rambling now. I could hear myself going on and on. I wanted to make sense of the situation. I think I realised that it was something magical that had happened.

"We'd already decorated his bedroom before he died. Grey and cream and a deep blue feature wall," Sue whispered as she stood up and came to me and wrapped her arms around me and we cried together, both missing a man called Alex.

Six months later…

It is amazing what you could achieve when you set your mind to it.

Shortly after my return from Menorca, I handed my notice in at the university. I was very scared at what lay ahead but I've received such encouraging remarks from everyone I knew. There were lots of comments such as, 'You should've done this ages ago', and 'Why did it take you so long?'. People at the uni, especially Val, were really loathed to see me go, but they wished me well with my new adventure. I'd paid back the money that I owed Val.

Val is now pregnant with twins! The final round of IVF worked. She's got two for the price of one! She's due in a couple of months, so not long now. I couldn't wish motherhood on a nicer person. She's going to be a brilliant mum.

I set up my new business under the name of 'Altered Images'. I did the pictures for Tracey's wedding, as promised, and the pictures were a big hit. Tracey and Carl loved them and they've let me use them to advertise my new business. I'm already starting to make a good income from the work I've done, and my books are steadily filling with orders.

I started working from the front room of my flat, but quickly began to realise I needed more space. I've rented a small shop in Heworth, not far from my flat, which makes the commuting time quite short. It isn't a very big space, but it suits my needs at the moment. I might need to get somewhere bigger at some point in the future, you never know!

Mum and I had made up as soon as I got back from Menorca. She was with Dad, waiting at the airport for me in arrivals. This time, she didn't have my name on a piece of card. As I came round the corner, we saw each other and I ran to her and gave her the biggest hug ever. I never want to fall out with Mum again.

As for Alex, I never heard from him again (surprise!), probably because he didn't exist. I think I've accepted that now. Sue and I have stayed in contact and I meet up with her every month or so. We've become quite close and often share stories about Alex. I think she realises that I know too many little details about him and his life for me not to have met him. Neither of us quite understand what really happened during that hot week in June.

When I think back to the week I shared with Alex, I close my eyes and I can still feel him, I can still smell him, I feel this touch on my skin. It HAD seemed real. I know I didn't imagine it.

I still believed it happened.